Stop and catch myse   l
stumbling off that bus   .
Only this is a different me. My hands and eyes are
the same, but I've changed. This is real and I'm
scared, but I'm doing it. This isn't rubber bands
and toy soldiers on the bedroom floor. This is me
and friends occupying TJ de Barra's island,
creeping up on Deathrow Dobbs's house.

'Don't flinch now . . .' murmuring aloud. 'Don't
flinch, Lynch.'

'That's what we'll call you, if we get through
this,' whispers Blaise. 'No-Flinch Lynch.'

'I suppose it's better than No-Puke Luke,' says
I, and all at once we're bursting with suppressed
giggles, bent over trying to keep it in, all the
tension, the craziness of this operation.

NO-FLINCH LYNCH

Jonathan Kebbe

Corgi Yearling Books

NO-FLINCH LYNCH
A CORGI YEARLING BOOK 0440 865093

Published in Great Britain by Corgi Books,
an imprint of Random House Children's Books

This edition published 2003

1 3 5 7 9 10 8 6 4 2

Papers used by Random House Children's Books are natural, recyclable
products made from wood grown in sustainable forests. The manufacturing
processes conform to the environmental regulations of the country of origin.

Set in 12/14pt New Century Schoolbook by
Falcon Oast Graphic Art Ltd.

Corgi Books are published by Random House Children's Books,
61–63 Uxbridge Road, London W5 5SA,
a division of The Random House Group Ltd,
in Australia by Random House Australia (Pty) Ltd,
20 Alfred Street, Milsons Point, Sydney, NSW 2061, Australia,
in New Zealand by Random House New Zealand Ltd,
18 Poland Road, Glenfield, Auckland 10, New Zealand,
and in South Africa by Random House (Pty) Ltd,
Endulini, 5A Jubilee Road, Parktown 2193, South Africa

THE RANDOM HOUSE GROUP Limited Reg. No. 954009
www.kidsatrandomhouse.co.uk

A CIP catalogue record for this book is available from the British Library.

Printed and bound in Great Britain by
Cox & Wyman Ltd, Reading, Berkshire.

To John and Georgia
– with love

Lorcan Lynch would like to thank the following
for their invaluable help in telling my story:
Rory O'Leary, John Wall, Tim Dunne, Mary and
Peter Carey, Mylene Laurin, Sue Cook,
Sophie Nelson and all the other freedom-fighters
on the Uxbridge Road

Never doubt that a small group of committed citizens can change the world.

Margaret Mead

PART ONE

SMASH THREE WINDOWS

Dad's in trouble again, dragged away by the police on the main evening news. Everyone in school looking at me like I've ten heads.

'Miss! *Miss!* You seen the news?' cries Matty Walsh the minute Miss Hart walks in.

Peering over her specs, *'No!'*

'But, miss, didn't you see whose dad was on telly?'

'The only thing I want to see, Mathew, is you getting down to work. Answer your names – Kevin Costello?'

Mind drifting, breathing deteriorating, worrying about Dad going to jail and Mum going off round the world again. Classmates staring at me.

'Lorcan Lynch? Wake up, please.'

'Sorry – here, miss.'

Ratty Matty making faces and tut-tutting, like I'm supposed to feel ashamed about Dad. Try thinking of something else, but keep re-playing TV images of burly cop saying,

Are you coming peacefully, Mr Lynch? and Dad replying, *Certainly not!*

'You OK?' best mate Gerry whispering.

A few eejits pass remarks in the playground, because it's not every day a TD – member of the Dáil, our parliament – gets arrested. Dad's an independent TD, and to many he's a troublemaker, shoving his nose in other people's business. To others he's a hero, sticking up for the little guy against dodgy employers and crooked building contractors who pay badly and disregard the safety of their men. Tomorrow he's in court. Some bookies even offering bets – *Teddy Lynch 4–1 to go down!*

Mates kicking a ball around: 'You playing, Lorcan?'

But the breathing's not so good, and I'm reaching for my inhaler when Mr LaCoste saunters over. Mr Lucky, we call him – tall black man from England via St Lucia in the Caribbean. He's taught us to play cricket!

'How you doing, Lorcan?'

'Fine, sir.'

'Not letting all the media attention get to you?'

'Just a bit.'

'Friday's match will take your mind off things.'

'My breathing's not so good this week, sir.'

10

'Your spirit's strong –' looking into my eyes – 'you'll be fine.' Pats me on the shoulder and walks away.

Ratty Matty swinging by for another dig, singing, 'Whose daddy's going to ja-ail?'

'Least I got one.'

Blood drains from his face.

Bus into town with Gerry and the gang. Usually I'm full of chat, but I'm shaky today and the traffic's bad, and panic is slipping its fingers round my throat. *Come on, come on!* Want to get home and lie down.

Dumped in the heat and dust of the city, and still another bus to catch.

'Don't worry, Lorky,' Gerry says as we get off. 'Bet you anything your dad walks free.'

'Bet you anything he doesn't!' Matty Walsh again. 'He's a disgrace and he's going down.'

'What do you bet?' says I.

'Fiver!'

'Tenner.'

'Done.'

Smack hands.

'See you tomorrow, Lorky.'

'See you, Gerry.'

Second bus packed as merry hell. Standing on the jammed lower deck, panic stroking my throat. Bus starting and stopping . . . rooting out my inhaler, scrunched up in the crush, to take a pull. Roads choked, air in the windows hot with chemicals, shirt sticking to me, I can't breathe . . . Where's Miss Hart? Where's Mum? I'm going to go under any second, drown at people's feet. Quick! Think of something else – Sadie waiting to jump up and lick my face when I get in . . . Hitting a hundred for Mr Lucky on Friday— Is this my stop? No, only the church –

Another pull on my inhaler. Two more stops – breathe, Lorcan, breathe! People looking at me like I'm crazy – let me off, quick! Squeezing towards the exit, bus inching forward, swaying to a stop. Open those flaming doors!

Stumble into the air, catch myself on a fence. Shuffle off into shady avenues, panic slipping its grip, vision clearing, lungs pumping – brilliant! I didn't go under. The demons didn't beat me. Once they gang up in big enough numbers around my lungs, I'm paralysed. And there's no escaping them. I've lived with these demons all my life. For days they're quiet and I feel fine, but they're always there, waiting, taunting me: *You're our prisoner, you belong to us! You're not like other kids, you're vulnerable and sickly – we can stop you any time, and one of these days we might even kill you.*

Well, you didn't get me today, did you! No, like Mr Lucky says, I got spirit, I got fight. Try as hard as you like, demons, I still play a cracking game of football, rugby, cricket – you name it. For the first half-hour or so anyway.

Happy, wildly happy.

Turn into my street, broad, calm, chirpy with birdsong. Thinking about apple juice and ice, when a man and a woman jump from a car across the street – coming towards me like in gangster movies. She's smiling and digging out a mobile; he's scruffy and pulling a gun! No, a camera. And not a mobile, a pocket tape recorder.

'Hi! Lorcan, isn't it? I'm Jacinta, this is Steve. Mind if I ask a few questions?'

Gazing stupidly at them.

'It is Lorcan, isn't it, Teddy Lynch's son?'

'Never heard of him.'

'You're not Lorcan Lynch?'

'I think I know my own name.'

'And what name would that be, if you don't mind my—?'

'Che Guevara!' says I, my dad's hero.

Don't know much about Che Guevara, except he was a Latin American freedom fighter whose family name was Guevara *Lynch*, like ours, but the pretty reporter and her ugly cameraman think it's funny.

'See you, Che!' they laugh as I stroll on, trying to look relaxed, when my legs are still shaky and I long to lie down. Walk on past my house and round the corner. Quick! Duck into Mrs Devine's drive and climb a wall. Know all these gardens: which hedge has a hole, which neighbour you can trust and which to avoid, like Mr Ledhammer – or Headbanger, as I call him. Well-known barrister, hates my dad. Pick my way carefully across his garden till I'm looking into mine, and there's Sadie dozing under the laburnum.

Hop over and Sadie's up and giving me her best wolfhound bark and a good licking.

'Get down, you're wrecking my uniform! Is Mum in?'

Silly question, she's never in. Raid fridge for juice and collapse at kitchen table. Gulp iced juice and lean back exhausted, cursing my demon-infested lungs. Will I ever be free of them? That's what I want to know. Mum's going away on work; Dad's in trouble – I'm scared, really scared.

Maria upstairs singing in Portuguese. The place is a tip – can't believe she hasn't quit like all the others. Boxes, files, stacks of newspapers, tower blocks of books, rows of jars waiting to be recycled. Friends go, 'Wow, it's so untidy!'

They're so busy, my parents, they pass like ships in the night. *Love you* – kiss-kiss! *See you soon!* They do their best to be there for me, but I spend more time with Maria, who started out a cleaner and now runs the show. She's not exactly beautiful, but I love her black smiling eyes. I love teasing her: 'Face it, Maria, Brazil are useless.'

'What means useless?'

'A team of window dummies could beat them.'

Looks up 'window dummies', and chases me round the house with a mop. Catches me, pins me down, 'Brazeel bestest in whole world – zay it, you bad boy!'

'All right, all right – Brazil's bestest in whole world!'

'Zank you!' Lets me go.

'Best at nuts and coffee, but useless at football!' The chase is on again!

Maria appearing now with a pile of washing: *'Oi, menino'* – hi, little guy – 'you make me fright! How you come in?'

'Smashed down the door – I'm Che Guevara.'

'Really! Nice to meet you, Che.'

Watch her loading the machine, wearing a number ten T-shirt with Brazilian star RIVALDO on the back.

'How you in school today?'

'Nearly got into a fight over Dad.'

'But you no fight?'

'No, I avoid fights.'

'Void?'

'A-void. Stay away from.'

'Are you feel OK?' Cool hand on my forehead. 'Don't worry, your father not go to jail.' Stroking my hair, 'You want I call his mother?'

'You mean *your* mother.'

'*My* mother?'

'It's *your* mother, if you're addressing me. Yes, we better warn her the press are outside.'

'Sorry, I have to go.'

'Don't worry. You get to your class.'

Making herself pretty in a mirror. The thought of Maria in some smoothie's arms makes my hackles rise.

'Is there someone in the class you fancy?'

'*Fancy?*'

'Is there a boy – a man, in your class?'

'Yes, there is woman and man.'

'But is there one like – you know, a boyfriend?'

'Boyfriend, in my English class? No!' She laughs. Putting on her denim jacket, checking for her bus pass. 'You little bit jilliz?'

'Jealous? *Nah* – yes!'

'No worry, *querido*, they not nice looking like you. Please say good luck to his father tomorrow.'

'You mean your father.'

'*My* father?'

'No, *my* father is *your* father when you're talking to me about him.'

Big sigh. 'My English go more worse, I think.'

Look out the window: Maria running down steps into an ambush – Beauty and the Beast hassling her for scandal on Dad. Shrugging and smiling. They could be asking the way to Mars for all she knows.

Sadie flinging her lead at my feet.

'Give me a break, Sadie, I got no breath.' But who can resist those pleading eyes? 'OK, OK, come on!'

Grab back-door key and run out the front. Sadie on short lead so she doesn't drag me under a car, or tie up a bus queue. Holding her back, sneaking a look round the hedge. Beauty and the Beast walking off with Maria, still trying their luck.

'This way, Sadie. *Whoo*, girl – slow down!'

Rapid stumbling walk round the park and back, and – *damn!* – they're still here, sitting in their car across the street.

'Sadie, wait for me at the door – I'll be five minutes. Go on.'

Duck into Mrs Devine's drive, where a car is now parked. No problem – ring bell. Mrs Devine in summer dress and trainers: 'Lorcan, what a pleasant surprise!'

Panting, 'Sorry, Mrs Devine, we got reporters again.'

'Oh, you poor things,' showing me out the back. 'Tell your dad we're rooting for him.'

'Thanks, Mrs Devine.'

Dragging myself through prickly hedge into Mr Headbanger's garden, getting ready to— *Oops!* It's him, the man himself, baggy shorts and knobbly knees, practising his golf swing.

'What on earth . . . ?'

'Hello, Mr Ledhammer, locked myself out again.'

'You've got reporters again, you mean, haven't you?'

Sidestepping across the garden, 'Thanks – bye.'

'If your father behaved in a manner you'd expect from a TD . . .'

Up onto his rockery I scramble and over the fence onto Mum's compost heap. In the back door and run to let Sadie in. 'Good girl, brave girl!' hugging her and getting another sticky licking, a few more stray hairs in the lungs.

How can you let him keep that dog? people keep asking Mum.

He wanted one so badly.

But why do you give in?

You try saying no when your son's fighting for his life.

Microwaved dinner in front of the TV. There's Dad on two flipping news channels, outside the Dáil, microphones shoved in his face. Switch to cartoons – quick! – before he punches someone else.

Mobile ringing – Mum, all breathless: 'On my way home, sweetheart, soon as I hail a— Hang on! Taxi! *Taxi!* Blind as a bat!'

Reminds me of a joke I sent Gerry: *Did you*

hear the one about the asthmatic wh
onto the street and inhaled a taxi!

She's an environmentalist, my mum.
environ-*mental*-ist, as I call her. She's a .y
Saturday, another round-the-world dash –
Bonn, Rio de Janeiro, Washington. Back for a
week and off again – Stockholm, Sydney,
Tokyo, leading an international delegation
trying to persuade governments to put
preservation of the planet before the pursuit
of profit – SEEDS BEFORE MISSILES! AIR BEFORE
OIL! NEED BEFORE GREED!

God help the politicians and business
leaders she runs into, 'cos when her wit
doesn't work, she turns tigress! I've heard her
on radio debates starting out friendly and
then – *Grrrrr! What do you mean you're doing
your best? I've seen better public transport in the
Sahara!* Seen her in TV debates sweet as pie,
suddenly rounding on a government minister:
You've got children, Mr So-and-so, haven't you?

*Yes, indeed, I've been blessed with a son and
two daughters.*

*Delighted to hear it – only what will you
reply when your children turn round one day
and ask, 'Daddy, how could you let our
beautiful world be ruined?'*

She does the same abroad. I think they give
in just to get rid of her. *All right, Mrs Lynch,
wind farms, wave power, free public transport
– anything you say – just leave us alone!* I

tease her, but I'm proud of her, the way she cares so much, the way she picks herself up after every defeat. Only sometimes, when she's away too long and the line's bad from Beijing or Kiev or God knows where, I feel like yelling, *For God's sake, Ma, come home and tuck me in!*

Lie down in my room with the blinds shut, nice and cool, letting the lungs settle. Then pick myself up and rattle through maths, French and a chapter on Napoleon's Russian campaign, and I'm switching on the computer to play Ireland versus Brazil when a taxi pulls up. Mum struggling out with shopping and dry cleaning – smack into Beauty and the Beast.

Run down to help. Mum's a big, wide woman, swatting them like wasps, but wasps don't give up. Hold back Sadie, who's howling with excitement!

'Mrs Lynch, what do you think of your husband hitting a security guard?'

Huffing and puffing up the steps, 'He wouldn't hurt a fly without a good reason.'

'You approve of his violence then?'

'Ted's his own man,' reaching the top and tottering indoors.

'Thank you, Mrs Lynch.' And then, seeing me, 'Ah, Che Guevara!'

'Yes! And you can tell your readers Dad's never going to jail,' says I, closing the door. '*Adiós!*'

Mum's reeling under Sadie's frantic welcome. 'What's all that about Che Guevara?'

'Fishing for gossip, they were, Ma. *You're Lorcan Lynch*, they said, *aren't you?* and I said, *No, I'm Che Guevara.*'

Expect her to laugh, but she catches her breath and looks at me. 'We have to talk.'

Don't like the sound of that, or the way she sits me down saying, 'I bought two tubs of pistachio ice cream to cheer us up . . .' pushing one towards me and grabbing two spoons. Then she goes, 'Look at the state of me! Stuffing my face, and all those dying children!'

'You're fine, Ma, you look great, and the ice cream would melt before it got to them.'

'Forty thousand a day, Lorcan.'

'I know, Ma.'

'All this global wealth and forty thousand children die needlessly every day.'

'I know, Ma, and you're doing your best.'

I worry about her extra bulk – it can't be good for her. But Dad likes her that way, says there's more to cuddle. She's big as a whale, he's thin as a pin, disappears into her when they hug.

'What's wrong, Ma?'

Sits me down, grabs my hand, frightening me. 'All this hullabaloo isn't good for you, so your dad and I have decided—' Car in the drive, Mum bustling to the front door.

Look out the window: it's Dad.

He's balancing files, locking the car, Beauty
pestering him, the Beast snapping pictures,
and here we go again – TV crews with woolly
microphones spilling from cars, stampeding
into the drive and up the steps. 'How you feeling, Mr Lynch?'

'Pretty good, thanks.'

'Think you can beat the rap tomorrow?'

'Do my best.'

'Does the prospect of jail frighten you, Mr
Lynch?'

'You kidding? I'm terrified!'

'Let my husband through!' Mum agitated.
'And mind what you're doing with that
microphone!'

'Do you think your husband will get off
tomorrow, Mrs Lynch?'

'Hope so, the grass needs cutting.'

'Thanks for coming!' Dad battling up the
final steps. 'See you in court!'

Me closing the door on the mob as Mum

pulls Dad inside and hugs him. Sadie trying to lick Dad's face, Dad ruffling my head. 'How you doing, kiddo? How's the breathing?'

'Threw a bit of a wobbly today.'

Dad and Mum exchanging looks. 'Sit down, Lorrie, we got to talk.'

They sit facing across the kitchen table, me piggy in the middle, Dad wiping his brow, Mum panting, Sadie flaked out on the floor.

'Some scrum, back there, eh, Lorrie!'

'They going to put you away, Dad?'

'Listen, if I go down, I'll cope. It's you we're concerned about, with me gone and your ma halfway round the world. Remember what we said: if things ever got too hectic—?'

'You're sending me away. Where?'

'To the West, to your Aunt Peig in Kilraine.'

'She'll take good care of you –' Mum's eyes filling up – 'and the Connemara air will clear your lungs.'

'And you'll be free of all this pandemonium,' Dad patting my hand.

'You'll have the time of your life, I know you will,' Mum patting my other hand.

'It's where our ancestors are from, rebels every one!' Dad's saying when the doorbell rings, reporters calling through the letter box –

'Excuse me, Mr Lynch, could we have a few words?'

'See what I mean? We're surrounded!'

'But Aunt Peig's mad, and lives in the middle of nowhere.'

Dad laughing, 'I never said she was mad.'

'You call her my Aunt Loopy.'

'She's my sister and she's one in a million.'

'What about her needles and potions and Che Guevara hat?'

'Beret, you fool. Che Guevara wore a beret!'

'Peig's always been *mad* about you, Lorcan,' says Mum.

'We never see her. I don't even remember what she looks like!'

'We're too busy to visit, and she hates Dublin.'

'But you said she doesn't even have a TV!'

'That's true,' says Dad.

'But everyone has a TV!'

'No, not everyone. And it'll be a change from all the mind-numbing pap you watch every night. It'll be good for you. Life's too cushy here. Your ma spoils you rotten.'

'Because of his asthma!'

'I'm not criticizing. I just don't want Lorcan growing up believing life is a shopping mall, and that the only heroes in the world are money-grabbing footballers and phoney pop stars. I don't want him growing up brain-washed like the rest of today's kids.'

'Easy now, Ted, not so hard.'

'So when am I going?'

Why is no one saying anything? Why are they looking at me like that?

'Tomorrow,' whispers Mum.

'Tomorrow?'

'I'm sorry, sweetheart, but—'

'You promised I could go to court.'

'And watch your dad grilled in front of all those people?'

'I want to support him.'

Looking at each other, eyebrows talking.

'How long am I going for?'

'Depends on your health, and how things calm down here.'

'What about school, and friends?'

Mum reaching for my hand again, 'You're going to a new school, a mixed school! That'll be fun, girls in the class.'

'What about Sadie?'

'She can stay with Maria or go with you. Peig says Sadie's welcome. She has a house full of strays.'

'So she won't mind you and Sadie, will she?' Dad trying to be funny.

'You've both had this planned for ages.'

'We were hoping it wouldn't come to this.'

'What's the school like?'

Mum hesitating, 'It's a state school. There's no independent one near. It won't be for long.'

'If I'm going tomorrow, that means I'm all done with Hadley Wood! I've already left! No chance even to say goodbye –' eyes stinging –

'I want to come to court tomorrow! And go to school on Friday. One last day.'

Dad spreading his hands, 'Sure, why not?'

Mum nodding frantically, 'Yes, that sounds better.'

Slope off to soak in a bath, lie back in a daze.

We're sending you to the West – a new school – a mixed school!

Sadie reaching over to lap dirty water.

'Sadie, listen to me –' looking up with big dopey eyes – 'how would you like to visit my nutty aunt in the wilds of Connemara?'

She gives a low, soft growl, beats the floor with her tail.

Into pyjamas and on line. One incoming message from Gerry. Aloud to Sadie, who tilts her head to listen: '*Hi, Lorky, check this: In Sunday School, Liam learned that God created Eve out of Adam's ribs. Days later, Liam's ma found him rolling around gripping his ribcage. What's wrong, son? It hurts here, Ma – I think I'm going to have a wife!*'

Laughter – not me; Dad in the doorway. 'Mind if I come in?' Standing over me, 'I hope I wasn't too hard on you earlier?'

'I know you want to be proud of me, Dad.'

'I *am* proud, but there's more to life than PlayStation, designer gear and football.' Picking up a GAP sweatshirt, 'I mean, look at this. Is it attractive? Colourful? Original?'

Shrugging, shrinking into myself.

'Lorrie, companies normally pay fortunes to advertise, but when you wear GAP or NIKE splashed across your chest, you're doing the advertising for them. And are they paying you? No, you're paying them! So who's the fool?'

'I don't think about things like that.'

'That's my point. Most important thing in life is to think for yourself.'

'You sure you don't mean to think like you, Dad?'

'No! Whatever you think is fine, long as your views are yours, not spoon-fed by TV. You got to decide: *Do I want to be free-thinking Lorcan Lynch, or one more brainwashed Coca-Cola kid who troops to McDonald's wearying the same uniform and thinking the same thoughts as everyone else.*'

He's upset, I'm upset.

'You really despise me, don't you?'

'Of course not! It's just that I don't want to lose you.'

'What do you mean?'

'Don't want to watch you swallowed up in the crowd. Look, Lorcan, there are two kinds of people in this world – active and passive, doers and dopes! You're one of those with the potential to shine, to amaze people, to improve the world.'

'Like Che Guevara.'

Laughing,'Well, you don't have to go that far. I just want you to be you! The full Lorcan. That's all. But now you mention him, you do have something vital in common with Che apart from the Lynch connection.'

'His asthma.'

'The attacks were so bad sometimes, his men had to carry him.'

'I know.'

'And you know something else, Lorrie? His asthma made him stronger than other men. Just as yours potentially makes you stronger.'

Dad perching on my desk, meeting my eye, 'Ever since you were little, Lorrie, I've marvelled how you threw yourself into sport, tried harder than anyone else, never giving in. Guevara was the same, a sickly kid who had to be taken out of school and sent away, but never let his asthma stop him doing anything. He'd play rugby like the furies the first half, knowing he'd have no breath left for the second. He cycled all over South America, and went on to become a dazzling guerrilla commander and statesman.'

Touching my shoulder, 'If I'm hard on you sometimes, it's because I don't want you losing that gritty spirit of yours. Do you understand?'

'I think so.'

'Think positively about Connemara. It'll be a real adventure.'

Humming as he leafs through my homework, 'Ah, Napoleon. Interesting, huh?'

'Very.'

'There's someone who did his own thing.'

'You mean he didn't wear a Nike sweatband riding into battle?'

Clicking his fingers, 'Just remembered! How would you like to meet him?'

'Who?'

'Napoleon! Been meaning to introduce him to you for years. Don't go away!' Skipping onto the landing, pulling down the attic ladder and climbing. Boards creaking above – what's he looking for? A Napoleon figurine? A fancy-dress costume? The man himself preserved in formaldehyde!

Here he comes lugging a trunk, a glint in his eye like a pirate. Throws open the trunk, releasing a musty smell. 'Want a peek at my past? Look! Matchbox cars inherited from your grandad. And Dinky cars of my own – Triumph Herald, Renault Dauphine, Jag with diamond headlights . . . encyclopaedias, atlas, marbles, cassettes: The Who – ever heard of them?'

'Who?'

'Exactly! School reports – December 1975: *Edward works well in bursts, but chats too much!* Ah, here we are . . .' unearthing a big white box tied with twine. Struggling with teeth and fingernails.

'You got Napoleon's bones in there, Dad?'

'I've got his whole army . . .' lifting the lid. Toy soldiers, hundreds of them! 'Recognize anything?'

'Waterloo!'

Cardboard strips divide the box into sections – French, British, Prussian. Their uniforms are precisely painted, down to belts, brasses and bayonets. Each section has its own mounted leader – stocky little Napoleon, upright Wellington and the cunning Prussian general, Blücher, plus complements of horse-drawn guns, hospital tents, wagons, feeble plastic trees and ruins.

'Ah, the official rules!' opening a booklet bound with string, filled with diagrams and instructions. Leather cup and dice.

'What are the dice for, Dad?'

'I forget exactly. It's in the rules.'

'What are these for?' Two steel rulers, one normal, one longer; collection of thick and thin rubber bands.

'It's all coming back,' grabbing a rubber band, stretching it over a ruler – *snap!* Tries another, and another; they all snap! 'Urgent mission, Lorrie! Find elastics while I set the scene.'

Run downstairs and hunt for rubber bands. Mission accomplished, return to an amazing sight: Wellington's men and guns deployed in brilliant red and white in the shadow of the sofa bed; Napoleon's forces in blue fanning out along the rug in the centre of the room; Dad on one knee, loosening his tie, hiding the Prussians under my desk.

'What are they doing under there?'

'Blücher didn't arrive till late, remember – Sadie, no!'

Whoops – too late, Sadie sliding over the smooth floor, massacring half the French flank.

'Sadie, you clumsy thunderbolt, that's historical nonsense!'

Dad whistling to himself as he selects a slim rubber band, stretches it the full length of the smaller ruler and, crouching behind the British lines, squints along the barrel. Now using his thumbnail, he carefully lifts the taut elastic to the very edge and – *whoosh!* – elastic flies, misses the French and drops harmlessly under the window. 'Call that marksmanship, you fools! I'll have you all court-marshalled!' – seizing the longer ruler and a thick elastic, hops behind Napoleon's lines to take aim at the British.

'There was heavy rain on the eve of the battle, and Napoleon's famous cannon were useless, but we won't worry about that . . .' – squinting along the ruler, stretching the taut elastic and – *Whoosh!* A pair of dragoons go flying. *'Bravo! Formidable!* You Eeengleesh are completely useless!'

Looking up flushed with joy, and a bit sheepish, 'Are we too old for this, Lorrie?'

'No, I don't think so.'

'Great! Who do you want to be – the Iron Duke, or good old Boney?'

Hadley Wood, Dad's court case, Connemara – all's forgotten. Nothing exists but the unfolding battle, closely observed by Sadie, who now and then stretches out a paw and chops down an unsuspecting grenadier.

3

Morning – looking out the window expecting to see reporters, but all's quiet.

'They'll be lying in wait outside the court,' says Dad over breakfast, his smiling face on the front of nearly every newspaper.

No school today, I'm off to court!

Here we go, all dressed up, piling into a taxi and crossing the traffic-choked city to the famous law courts on the quays. Dad in fine form: 'Should be a good crack today, folks!'

Mum tense, wheezing worse than me: 'Just be nice to the judge, Ted, and stay out of jail.'

Soon as we stop, we're caught in a crush of supporters, press and police – laughter, shouts, clicking cameras.

'Give us a smile, Ted! ... Give 'em hell, Teddy!'

Part of me feels like a film star's son, the other part wonders why I can't have normal parents like everyone else. Reminds me of one of Gerry's jokes: *Mummy, Mummy, can I lick*

*the bowl? No, you'll pull the chain like any
normal child.*

Courtroom's packed, echoing with Dad's
rowdy constituents. Security guard Jason
Booth takes the stand, brute with shaven
head. Pointing at Dad, 'He hit me, *twice*! I
needed medical attention and was off work for
a week.'

Jeers from the gallery: 'Ye big softie!'

Whispering to Mum, 'He's twice as big as
Dad.'

'Keep your fingers crossed.'

Prosecution calling another witness, Jack
de Barra, chairman of Galaxy Holdings.

'One of Dad's mortal enemies –' Mum
whispering – 'and would you believe, he has a
summer home on an island five minutes from
Aunt Peig in Kilraine.'

Let's hope I don't run into him, I'm thinking, as handsome Jack de Barra takes the
stand, and starts slating Dad in a smooth,
husky voice –

'It's beyond belief than an elected member
of the Dáil would encourage his constituents
to rampage through my offices, using carpets
as ashtrays, and changing nappies on the
boardroom table!' Jeers and laughter. 'They
may find it amusing, Your Honour, but I'm
sure most decent people would agree that a
spell in jail might help reform our wayward
TD.'

'Booo . . . booo!'

Judge frowning, 'Thank you, Mr de Barra, but if I need your help in sentencing, I'll ask for it.'

Dad taking the stand, Mum squeezing my arm. His beaky-looking barrister sends half the courtroom to sleep, but Dad's replies are crisp and confident, and I'm sure he'll get off.

'The proposed office block and leisure centre would cast my constituents into eternal shadow. It would be like living beneath the Cliffs of Moher with windows in it!' Thumping applause! 'And the new access road would put a complete stop to children playing on Dolphins Green. As for the compensation Mr de Barra is offering for ruining their environment, it would make Scrooge blush!'

Loud cheers! 'You tell 'em, Ted!'

'And regarding the way they've been harassing my constituents with threats, such as – I quote – *You better take the money, or we'll bury you!* I can only say that the executives of Galaxy Holdings make the Taliban look like gentlemen!'

Thunderous applause all round the gallery!

'Objection!' roars the opposition barrister, pompous fellow with sarky tone. 'That's an outrageous slur on the good name of my clients! What's more, you're evading the issue, Mr Lynch.'

The judge agrees. She's losing patience.

'This case isn't about Galaxy Holdings,' sighs Sarky-face, 'but about your conduct, sir, when, by your own admission, you led an occupation by unruly elements among your constituents and turned violent when ordered to leave. Do you deny assaulting Jason Booth, Mr Lynch?'

'He was assaulting a pregnant constituent of mine.'

'He was *escorting* her with considerable care from the premises, Mr Lynch.'

On and on it goes, Sarky-face attacking, Dad biting back, until suddenly the judge snaps and bangs her table, demanding to know whether Dad regrets the trespass and assault, and furthermore, 'Are you willing to reassure the court, Mr Lynch, that under no circumstances will you re-engage in such reprehensible behaviour?'

Mum patting my knee, 'She's giving him a way out.'

But Dad doesn't look sorry. 'With regret, Your Honour, I cannot apologize for defending my constituents. Nor can I promise not to go to their aid in the future.'

'In that case, you leave me no alternative but to sentence you to twenty-eight days for common assault, and a further twenty-eight for contempt of court!' *BANG!* Dismissed!

Jack de Barra's on his feet applauding, the gallery's up and booing, guards drawing truncheons, officers of the court leading Dad away.

But he's not finished, he's pulling back, addressing the crowd: 'Jack de Barra tried to frighten my constituents out of their homes – *he* should be on trial!' Roars of approval! 'Unfortunately, ladies and gentlemen, the law in this country favours the rich and ruthless—'

'That's enough, Mr Lynch!'

'Protects gangsters and profiteers!'

'I said that's enough!'

They're wrestling Dad from the room, but he's still shouting: 'And permits crocodiles in suits to gorge themselves on defenceless communities!'

Just time to throw us a smile as he's marched away.

Mum stunned, fighting back the tears. Faces turning to see her reaction.

Calm, smiling, 'Come on, sweetheart, lots to do.'

4

BANG! BANG! They're shooting at Dad! He's making a break for it across the cricket field – BANG! Stumbles, picks himself up and keeps going – BANG-BANG-BANG! – *'Dad!'*

Eyes open, wide awake! Where am I?

Bang! Bang! More newspapers hitting the hall floor below, and it all comes back: Dad in court yesterday, going down fighting.

'Lorcan?' Mum calling. 'It's getting late.'

Getting dressed in a daze. While I slept in my bed last night, Dad spent his first night behind bars. Mum's going to see him today. She might take me tomorrow, before I catch my train west and she her plane south.

Drops me at the number 7 stop for the last time for goodness knows how long.

'Good luck today, sweetheart. When we've done our packing later, we'll get a takeaway and watch a video or something, OK?' She means it, but somehow I doubt it'll happen.

Riding the bus out of town, monitoring my

38

breathing, fingering the inhaler. Here comes the sea on the left, Sandymount beach exposed by the tide, dotted with mussel-diggers and dog-walkers.

My stop. Last time for ages I'll walk this way, joining other boys trooping along the same streets in the same uniform. Attracting glances. Who cares! What Dad gets up to has nothing to do with me.

Sit at my desk, glance round at classmates I won't see till – when?

'You OK, Lorky?'

'This is my last day, Gerry.'

'What?'

Matty Walsh standing over me. Slap a ten-euro note in his palm.

'You must have heard the news this time, miss,' he goes, soon as Miss Hart appears.

'No, Mathew—' banging her bags down – 'I make a point of never listening to the news!'

Of course she's heard, that's why she's late, discussing with colleagues how best to deal with me.

Gerry staring at his open history book, me at mine, same paragraph over and over: *As winter overwhelmed Napoleon's army, many of his men fell asleep in the snow and never woke up . . .*

Belly all twisted up, breathing getting thinner.

'But, miss, I can't believe you're the only teacher in the world—?'

'Sit down, Mathew, or I'll be the only teacher in the world to murder a pupil in cold blood.'

Gales of laughter: 'Go on, miss, do it!'

She's trying to act normal, but she's avoiding my eye, like it's my fault my dad's hit the headlines with JAIL FOR REBEL TD and 56 DAYS' PORRIDGE FOR TEDDY LYNCH.

Hordes of little demons infiltrating my chest – pressing round my lungs.

I don't want to leave. I don't want to go to Connemara. I like Miss Hart and all the other teachers. I like my work and my friends. Everyone knows and respects me. They've seen me loads of times carried out to an ambulance, but I'm still Lorcan Lynch, captain of the soccer team, rugby team and debating team – the main man!

Breathing deteriorating, fingers tightening round my throat, thought of travelling to the far West, moving in with a stranger, starting a state school where they'll hate me 'cos I'm a snotty Dubliner with a jailbird dad. Miles from home.

Look out at the sports field, dual carriageway and the sea, and I want to cry, want to smash something. I belong here. Why should I leave just 'cos Dad's got himself banged up?

Chest clenched, breath squeezed dry –

someone trying to push my head under water. Reaching again for the inhaler – wrong pocket! Keep breathing – breathing – leaning down for another deep pull.

'Kevin Costello?' Miss Hart calling the register in a cheery tone.

Lungs scraping like sandpaper.

'Paul Flynn?'

'Here, miss.'

'Vincent Halliday?'

'Miss.'

'Lorcan Lynch?'

She's looking down at the register. I'm not answering if she won't look at me.

'Lorcan?' – meeting my gaze.

Mean to say, *Here, miss*, but can't squeeze the words out. Nod and keep reading . . . *and now his Grande Armée was reduced to vagabonds eating horseflesh washed down with snow . . .*

Breathing getting worse, everybody watching me, wondering how bad it's going to get. I'm not the only 'huffler', as we asthmatics are called. A couple of others are starting to wheeze, and someone's laughing, and that's catching too, and it's no good Miss Hart looking daggers, it's just nerves and, let's face it, it is funny, schoolboys sounding like old codgers ready to croak.

Miss Hart making eye signals at me: *You sure you're all right?*

Fine, I nod, loosening tie and opening shoulders, breathing deep and slow – deep and slow, trying not to hit the poison too often. Touch and go – everyone silently rooting for me – or not. Nothing like an asthma attack to stop work.

. . . reduced to vagabonds eating horseflesh washed down with snow . . .

Breathing like a blocked drain, the room beginning to spin. I'm like the guy in the Jack London story stranded in snowy wastes, fighting off starving wolves with flaming torches. Trying to distract the wolves with random thoughts: my surprise birthday pressie for Mum – a hanging basket! And the time Dad left the budget debate in the Dáil an hour early to see me in the school play; and the night they cried when Mum miscarried again, and I cried alone, 'cos it never crossed their minds it was my sister or brother they'd lost.

Wolves closing in . . . *eating horseflesh washed down with snow . . .*

Brisk knock on the door, enter Mr O'Toole, our principal.

Heart soars – he's come to tell everyone the good news that President McAleese has pleaded for clemency, and the Prime Minister has agreed to Dad's immediate release; I'm not leaving after all.

Miss Hart telling us to sit up. Mr O'Toole

smiling sadly, a priest at a funeral. 'Good morning, boys.'

'Morning, sir.'

'I regret to inform you that this is Lorcan's last day with us.' Gasps. 'He's going to a new school for a while – in Connemara, where the air is purer.'

Lungs not working, inhaler not working.

'It's a blow to me and all the staff, as I'm sure it is to you, though I hope it won't be for too long. But it's harder still for Lorcan, so I know you'll try and make his last few hours . . .'

Help! Groping for air, drowning! Sliding off the chair like a coat, hands diving to grab me before I hit the—

'Quick, boys!' Miss Hart calling the usual team to action – scooping me up, steadying me, carrying me out like a wounded comrade.

Oxygen! Sweet oxygen! Dozing in the sick room.

Someone's coming – Mum! Out of breath. 'I jumped in a taxi soon as I heard. You OK?'

'Fine.'

Taking my hand, 'Why didn't they call an ambulance?'

'Wasn't that bad.'

'How can I leave you when you're like this?'

Look who else is here – Mr Lucky, smiling sternly! 'Good afternoon, Mrs Lynch! Lorcan.

What's all this about being a little breathless? I hope you haven't forgotten our honour's at stake after that cruel defeat last week at the hands of those northern scallywags?'

'But I've missed it, haven't I?'

'Still playing, and we're in dire straits. They've agreed you can bat, so as soon as you're ready. Gentlemanly retribution is called for, with you, dear boy, leading the fight back!'

Mum amazed, 'Do you really think he's up to it?'

'Absolutely.'

Getting changed alone. Sit quietly a moment mastering the breath, and then shuffle light-headed, loose-limbed into the sunlight. Last few hours slipping through my fingers.

I like the way both sides play all in white, so we're all the same, a game more about playing than winning. I like Mr Lucky's sense of fair play, applauding when an opposition player makes a fine shot or brilliant catch, encouraging us to do the same. A gentleman's game! And what a day for it, sea glistening, breeze cooling my lungs. If only I wasn't so shaky, the ghost of that last attack still clinging to me.

Mr Lucky signalling me, *Hurry, you're in!* Pads fastened, walking out for the last time. We're sixty runs behind, the match effectively lost, Sir indicating, *Nice and steady*.

Nice and steady – the mood I'm in? Must be joking! I'm mad at my classmates for staying when I'm leaving, mad at Mr O'Toole and Miss Hart for letting me go, at Mum for preparing to abandon me, Dad for criticizing me, God for lumbering me with defective lungs. They're sending me away, and someone's got to pay!

Rage making my blood boil – *Slash! Sweep! Drive!* The ball flying in all directions, fielders scurrying like rabbits. Mr Lucky's smiling, and shaking his head: this is no way to play. Mum's waving enthusiastically from the boundary, answering her mobile at the same time. Should be signs saying, WILL PARENTS KINDLY REFRAIN FROM USING MOBILES, AS THEY TEND TO DISTRACT THE BATSMEN.

Reminds me of another of Gerry's e-mails: *Sign in butcher's shop in Wexford* – WILL CUSTOMERS KINDLY REFRAIN FROM SITTING ON THE MEAT SLICER, AS WE'RE GETTING BEHIND WITH OUR ORDERS.

Little crowd's buzzing, I'm scoring at such a gallop, we could even win. But I'm not interested in winning, I want to go out with a bang – and the sound of breaking glass: my classroom window, the staff-room window and, if possible – it's a long way off – Mr O'Toole's office window: drop a ball on his desk as he signs a farewell letter to my parents . . . *with best wishes, yours sincerely – CRASH!*

45

Classroom's sixty-odd metres away to my left and slightly behind me; it'll take nerve and precision. They're bringing on a tall, fresh bowler with a farcically long run-up, taking him ages to arrive and deliver a vicious bouncing missile – *duck*, ruffling my hair in its slipstream.

Mr Lucky, in his umpire's white coat, wags a finger. 'We don't want broken bones, do we!'

Villain shrugs, sniffs, hikes back to his mark. Lean on my bat taking in the view, the crowd, a parade of seagulls on my classroom – former classroom – roof.

Here comes Marathon Man kicking up the dust, leaping in the air and flinging down a hopelessly inaccurate ball, so inaccurate I nearly dislocate myself trying to reach it and miss completely.

Calm down ... patience, mimes Sir. Patience? What's he talking about?

Time to scratch an itch, flex my shoulders, wonder how Sadie's doing, while my adversary trudges into the haze, turns and comes again, trundling up and flinging down another missile – *SMACK!* That's it, hot out of the bat, curving high over the field, over Miss Hart and Mum, shielding their eyes, over the playground and down in a lazy, dipping roll towards – wait for it – *SMASH!* Clean through the classroom window, triggering an explosion of gulls.

Goodbye desk! Goodbye classmates! Goodbye Miss Hart!

Gasps from the boundary!

Gulls, blowing like litter, settle on the nearby staff-room roof. Big mistake.

Here he comes again, pounding up and hurling down another rocket which threatens – if I miss – to tear my stumps from the ground and hurl them into the sea. But I'm not in the mood to miss, not today! And eye glued to the ball, I step back, soften the wrists and *WHACK!* Away it flies, high over the bike shed and teachers' car park, dropping like a bird of prey – wait for it – *SMASH!* – clean through the staff-room window, gulls screaming in all directions.

Crowd erupts, Mum and Miss Hart clap hands over mouths in shock. Nervous faces appearing at the shattered window. Gulls retreating to the safer heights of Mr O'Toole's office. Safer? We'll see about that.

Crowd's excited: victory's in sight. But victory's the last thing on my mind. Gaze once more at my final goal, the principal's window, gleaming in the sun.

Marathon Man's really mad now, cheeks flushed, face and hair streaming, pounding up for another venomous – onto it in a flash – *CRACK!* Watch it climb like an arrow over the scoreboard, the running track and the care- taker's garden, commencing its descent above trees and the ornamental fountain to hit the target with an almighty – *Damn!* Overshoots and drops out of sight.

Another six; the crowd hoots for joy. Not I.

Last ball of the over, the crowd buzzing with anticipation, Mum shouting encouragement, opposition players glaring at me, trying in ungentlemanly fashion to put me off, but they're fools, because nothing – not a tidal wave, tornado or terrorist attack – is going to stop me today. And here he comes, thundering up and flinging down a final thunderbolt, a white-hot spinning blur coming at me so fast I've barely time to step back, lift the bat and – *THWACK!* – away it goes, over the twisting heads of the crowd, the running track, care-taker's garden and fountain, and into its long, smooth descent, down, down – *CRASH! Bingo!* Wonderful explosion of glass and sea-gull panic in the clear summer air.

Gulls whirling away into the distance.

What a feeling! Lungs pumping, blood on fire. Amazement in the crowd, Mr Lucky chuckling in disbelief – and look! Mr O'Toole, stomping out to investigate, and away trots Miss Hart to reassure him it's not some vile act of vandalism, but Lorcan Lynch turning the tide for Hadley Wood.

Ha!

Last over: six runs to win. Brief respite while my batting partner scrambles a run.

Five runs to win; five balls left. Their crafty spinner's on, juggling the hot ball, plotting my downfall. Crowd and team-mates urging me on, and I'd love to oblige, but I'm spent, lungs limp as a pair of punctured inner tubes. Here comes the wizard, skip, hop and a swirl of red coming out of the sea. Stride forth to meet it – *Damn!* Could have sworn it was going to turn into my legs, but instead it spins away. Flap helplessly and watch it clip the bat and shoot straight up in the air, hanging there so long, my executioner has time to wave his mates away, and place himself with open hands beneath it.

Ah well. Everybody's clapping and laughing, opposition, crowd, teachers – no one's ever seen anything like it – all except Mr O'Toole, who can't quite see the funny side of three broken windows.

Mum naturally offers to pay, but he won't hear of it. 'Let's call it a leaving present,' he says, looking at me strangely, wondering could I have possibly . . . ? No, surely not.

Time to say goodbye. Mr O'Toole shaking my hand warmly, 'We'll miss you, my boy.'

Miss Hart hugging me, 'Send us a postcard, or we'll never speak to you again!'

Mr Lucky's friendly arm around my shoulder, 'Interesting innings, Mr Lynch.' He knows! 'Keep it up. You've a great spirit!'

Mates don't know what to say, nor I.

Whacking me on the back, running off whistling and waving – 'See you, Lynchy! Don't break all the windows in your new school!'

Gerry holding the door for Mum. Taxi groans as she gets in. 'Bye, Mrs Lynch.'

'Goodbye, Gerry, take care. Lorcan won't be away long, I promise.'

Throw bags in, jump in and roll down the window.

'We'll e-mail each other every night,' says Gerry.

'Witches don't have PCs and mine's too big to take.'

'OK, we'll text.'

Drive away, friend and school shrinking in the mirror.

Mum laughing, 'One minute an asthma attack, the next you're stepping out for the school and breaking not one, not two, but –' giving me a funny look – 'Lorcan, you didn't . . . ?'

'Didn't what?'

'Do it on purpose?'

Blankly returning her gaze. Saved by her mobile.

Nearer home she sighs, 'How can I leave you like this?'

'I'm fine, Ma.'

'I'm seriously thinking about cancelling.'

'Don't be silly.'

'They'd just have to manage.'

'No one fights for the world like you.'

'You know I'll cancel, if you need me to.'

'I know.'

'Mind you, even if I stayed –' pulling up at our house – 'I could never protect you from all this.'

It's not that bad, I was going to say, when the cab's surrounded!

'Smile, sweetheart. They may look like hyenas, but they really are human.' Someone opening Mum's door. 'Thank you, you're a gentleman!' she says, climbing out and answering questions as we climb the steps.

'What do you think of your husband being sent down, Mrs Lynch?'

'He asked for it.'

'Weren't you shocked by the two-month sentence?'

'Yes, should have been far longer.'

Smiles and laughter. 'How will his sentence affect you, Mrs Lynch?'

'It'll save on grocery bills.'

'What about your son?'

'Leave my son out of it.' *Grrr!* The tigress. 'I'd invite you all in for tea and home-made brack, but you'd need your stomachs pumped.'

5

Indoors, Sadie goes mad. Mum ruffles her head and tells me, 'Your packing's done. Check I haven't missed anything. I haven't even started mine!'

Sadie throwing her lead at my feet.

'Not now, I've got—' *Homework to do*, I was going to say, forgetting I've done my last Hadley Wood homework.

'We might be on the news at six,' Mum calling.

Do I really want to see myself on the news?

Sadie follows me upstairs, nudging my bum with her big head.

'Sadie, I hate it when you do that!'

Dump school bags on the bed. Arms ache as I stretch to shove the cricket bat on top of the wardrobe.

Two suitcases lie open on the sofa bed, one topped with my bathrobe, pyjamas and cool see-through wash bag Mum bought yesterday, with the electric toothbrush that shouts,

Goal! and bursts into applause when it thinks you've brushed enough. Second case topped with my best suit. Dig deeper and find scarf, woolly hat and gloves!

'Ma! What's the suit for?'

'Never know when you might need it.'

'Gloves and woolly hat?'

'It can be pretty wild in Connemara, believe me.'

'What you really mean is I'm going to be there till Christmas.'

Stretch out on the floor, hands behind head. Last night in this house. New chapter about to begin. *It'll be an adventure – a real adventure.*

Spotting Dad's white box on the desk, get up and open it. Study the tattered instruction booklet. Set out men and artillery approximately as they were long ago, with trees, ruins and field hospitals. Standards fluttering in the breeze, hooves squelching, gunners cursing as heavy field pieces slide and sink and men's hearts go *bom-bom-bom*.

All else forgotten – it's dawn on the twenty-somethingth of June 1815, and the English are in deep manure.

'You Eengleesh poodles!' Napoleon jeers from headquarters between Sadie's paws. 'Surrender – or eat mud!'

'God bring me night, or bring me Blücher!' cries Wellington from the sofa-bed heights as I roll his last dice.

A six! 'Look, Sadie! Blücher's Prussians are on the march!'

Lifts her head, thinks it's time for walkies.

'Lorcan?' A dimly familiar voice from below. 'Dinner!'

It's 6.29 in the sunny suburbs of Dublin and, one hundred and eighty-odd years after the event, murderous French cannonades have scythed the 69th Foot and Scots Greys to shreds, and English fire has reduced Napoleon's Imperial Guard to a solitary shell-shocked chasseur facing the wrong way.

Window open, warm dusty air hanging like smoke. Reach for my inhaler as General Ney, Napoleon's bravest and stupidest marshal, sends a last desperate plea for reinforcements.

Napoleon throws a fit! 'Where ze 'ell am I to get more men from, you nincompoop, you *espèce de* horse poo?'

'Lorcan! Dinner's getting cold!'

Dinner? How can anyone think of food at a time like this? Fire! *Whoosh!* Amazing! Ney's horse shot from under him, exactly as in 1815. Fire! *Whoosh!* Napoleon's hit! He spins, totters, stays upright. *Incroyable!*

'He's alive, Sadie! *Vive Napoléon! Vive la France!'*

Napoleon's last throw. A five! 'Zat vill do nicely. OK, Meestair Welleengtonn, prepare to meet your makair!'

Vault battlefield, take up position behind Sadie's bum.

'Lorcan! It's getting stone cold!'

Stretch thickest elastic over biggest ruler, aim at imperious Iron Duke astride white charger on *Mont-Saint-Sofa Bed* and – What's that? Thunder on the stairs! Mum in the doorway, breathless –

'Lorcan, have your ears fallen off?'

Thumbnail quivering, Wellington swaying in my sights. 'Hang on, Ma. Europe's fate hangs in the balance.'

'So does yours!'

'Last shot.'

'Quickly.'

Settle once more, try not to let Sadie's thumping tail distract me and – *whoosh!*

'Shot!' Mum applauds as man and horse are swept to the floor.

'Yes! And with his last throw, Napoleon wins Waterloo and rewrites history!'

'Better tell your teacher to order new history books –' Biting her lip, 'Sorry, sweetheart, silly me.'

Leaving thousands of unburied bodies upstairs to be picked over by crows, we carry our dinners through to watch the news, and there we are, arriving with Dad at court! And here's Mum teasing reporters on our steps, me a right eejit all in white with green knees.

* * *

Sleep the deep sleep of the Window Smasher. Dream crazy dreams about trying to rescue Dad from prison, calling out in whispers, *'Dad, Dad, where are you?'* and him replying, *'Here, over here!'* and still I can't find his cell.

Wake in cold sweat with the covers thrown off.

Morning. Grey and drizzly. Maria in early to help finish packing. Me messing, tossing in silly things like toilet rolls and bath mat.

'Lorcan, you crazy bad boy!'

Running late, visiting Dad in jail, then Mum's dropping me at the station and herself at the airport. Mum shoving bags at the patient cab driver, Sadie jumping in the back, me throwing my arms around Maria's neck.

'Don't forget to write!' says I, knowing she can barely speak English, never mind write it.

'Até logo, querido' – bye, darling – zipping a little something into my pocket.

Mum bombarding her with final instructions and we're away. Turn and watch Maria shrinking on the steps. Mum's mobile going for the hundredth time this morning. Cuts it short – 'There!' smiling at me, full of worry.

Sadie looking out as we crawl in traffic. Mum wheezing worse than me – husband behind bars, son going West and she's flying away.

'It'll be OK, Ma, you'll see.'

Mum lurching out of her seat – 'Oh, driver, I'm so sorry, I forgot—!'

Driver distracted – hits brakes. Young woman crossing with baby buggy goes mad!

Mum shaking, waving apologies to the poor woman: 'Sorry, everyone – my fault.'

'Reminds me, Ma, of one Gerry sent me: *Keep death off the roads! Drive on the pavements!*'

Driver's laughing. 'You want me to turn round?'

'No, no! I forgot to ask: could you bear looking after Sadie while we go in?'

Pulling up outside the clean modern entrance. Glimpses of ancient accommodation blocks beyond, rows upon rows of barred windows. And look who's here to meet us. Beauty and the Beast!

'Morning, Che! Morning, Mrs Lynch! Visiting your old man?'

'How did you guess?'

'Something nice for him there?'

'Banana bread, his favourite.'

'Bake it yourself?'

'Yes, and with a forty-five in it, so he can shoot his way out.'

Present ourselves at fortified reception desk. Sit in airless waiting room jammed with visitors, sickly-looking women and teenage mums rocking infants and snapping at kids, chatting and smoking. Their coarse tongues and faces amaze me. Feel like a pedigree pup in a noisy dog pound. Smoke sticking like soot to my lungs.

Whispering, 'Not sure I want to go in.'

'You won't see him for quite a while.'

Someone recognizing Mum: 'Fair play to yer husband, missus! Imagine that cow sending him down for sticking up for ordinary people.'

'Should 'a' got a medal!' Laughter and solidarity.

'Your da's a good man, son' – woman lecturing me.

'Pity the rest aren't like him,' says another.

'In it for the'selves, so they are, but your da's different, God bless him.'

Dad's a hero. I'm proud and confused. We're being called.

'You want to wait here for me, Lorcan?'

'No, it's OK.'

Led in small groups through one security door after another, keys ringing, doors banging, voices echoing deeper into the prison. Place reeking of men, cabbage and cleaning fluid. Breathing thin, heart racing. Steered into bare room, uniformed men watching while females body-search us, examine Mum's fruit and books, poke holes in her cake. Can't help staring at it, waiting for a sticky .45 to emerge . . .

On we go, holding hands, into a big, echoing hall – high windows and basketball nets.

Visitors murmuring at wide tables facing lo.
prisoners in blue overalls, with hawk-eyed
warders round the walls.

'He's over there, Ma!'

Waving like he's meeting us off a plane.
Used to seeing him in suits or jeans. He looks
like a car mechanic.

We're allowed to hug. He's fresh-shaved and
drenched in cologne. Sit facing: Dad red-eyed
and pasty, a stranger. Laughs, 'Cheer up, me
hearties! You're both off on great adventures!'

'Dad, I don't like seeing you in here.'

'I'm on holiday! Regular meals, interesting
new friends.'

'How's the food, pet?'

'Brilliant, Maggie! Chefs flown in from
Paris' – screwing up his face to let me know
it's actually *horrible*.

'What's the new cellmate like?'

'Professional jewel thief. I'm teaching him
to read, he's teaching me to crack safes. Fair
exchange, don't you think?'

'Ted –' Mum sighing – 'how can I leave you
like this?'

'That's what she said to me, Dad!'

'What, another bad turn?'

'Didn't stop me playing cricket.'

'I was seriously thinking of cancelling,' says
Mum.

'Don't worry, Mags, he's going to have a
great time.'

'I hit four sixes, Dad.'

'And broke three windows!' says Mum.

'My classroom, the staff room and Mr O'Toole's office.'

Dad looking at Mum, who nods to confirm the historic feat.

'And we still lost!'

'Ah, but gloriously. Better to lose gloriously—'

'Than to win drearily. I do listen, Dad.'

'I wish *you'd* listened a bit more, Ted' – Mum softly. 'You promised to behave in court. It's very hard on Lorcan.'

'I know –' throwing his hands up in surrender – 'I'm sorry, Maggie. Sorry, Lorcan. Sometimes you have to put your principles first, even if it hurts your family. At least, I think so. Anyway, Lorrie –' big sigh – 'Connemara's going to be brilliant.'

'Long as I don't run into that horrible chairman of Galaxy Holdings who was so keen to see you jailed.'

'That's right, my old pal Jack de Barra owns an island down there.'

'I might just sail over and break his windows.'

'You do that, son. And while you're at it, smash up Willie-John McNulty's place – he's the local TD. He also lobbied vigorously for my imprisonment.'

'Ted! Don't encourage him.'

'Aren't you scared in here, Dad?'

'Why would I be?'

'Isn't the place full of . . . ?'

'Full of what, son?'

Whispering, 'Robbers . . . junkies . . . murderers?' afraid of being overheard by families visiting robbers, junkies and murderers.

Laughs, 'I meet worse every day in the Dáil!'

'Seriously, there must be loads of evil characters in here.'

Scratching his neck, 'There aren't many bad people in here – only people who've done bad things. A young man trying to provide for his girlfriend and kiddies panics when the landlord raises the rent again, does a wicked thing, robs a petrol station, goes to jail. Some would say his landlord is a worse criminal, robbing innocent people, driving them to despair. And while a young man who sells dangerous drugs to feed a desperate habit receives a big jail sentence, the nicely dressed businessman selling lethal weapons to murderous governments receives a big salary. The rich get richer – the poor get jail. You get my drift, son?'

Time's up. Mum and Dad clinging; Dad hugging me: 'Enjoy your adventure, Lorrie, and whatever you do – be yourself!'

Relief to get out in the air. Sadie thrilled to see us, making the cab shake.

'Heuston Station, please – quick as you can!'

Crawling along the quays.

'Relax, Ma, we'll make it.'

The station suddenly upon us. Running in, hunting for trolleys, Mum trying to ring Aunt Peig.

'The train to Galway will depart from Platform One, calling at . . .'

Asking permission to put me on board. The man replying, 'No problem, but that dog's got to go in the guard's van.'

You must be joking!

Train's packed, Sadie holding back. 'Come on, girl, pretend it's the Ark.' Dog lovers smiling at her – others looking sniffy.

'There's a seat, Lorcan – quick!'

'I need two, Ma! I'm not putting her in the guard's van.'

Pulling Sadie up the aisle, 'Hop up, girl!' Squeeze in beside her. Across from us, a stuffy woman and her podgy daughter about my age laying out a picnic. Woman sees Sadie, puffs her cheeks like a toad. Give her my best smile, but her face says, *What do you mean by inflicting that animal on us!*

People bumping and squeezing – where can we fit our bags? Sadie bewildered, hopping up and down, leaning into Mrs Toad, who flinches in horror.

'Sorry!' Mum smiling, but Mrs Toad's face

says, *How dare you allow him to bring that beast on board!*

Mum panting and pointing: 'Toilet's that way . . . don't forget your sandwiches . . . and here's a bit of extra cash for a rainy day . . .'

'Ma, get going.' She's going to have a heart attack.

Hugging me, hugging Sadie, squeezing the life out of us. Rubbing lipstick off my face. Tears in her eyes – 'Bye, sweetheart, love you.'

'Love you, Ma.'

Lean out, watch her getting smaller and disappear. She's gone, we're moving. Sit down, measure the breathing. Sadie jumping up, tossing her head. Dog hairs, real or imagined, drift towards enemy lines. Mrs Toad frantically covering cheese, dips, pickles.

Sadie sticking her head out the window, looking gloomily across the tracks. What's she thinking? Mum reckons she's not the brightest. Wandered into the road once and was hit by a van. I nearly died, driver jumped out white as a sheet, and just as I'm starting to break my heart crying, she hops up, shakes herself down and licks the driver.

Hate the thought of her missing her basket, Maria, the borzoi up the street. Whispering in her ear, 'We're going to Connemara – new sights and smells, dogs with funny accents . . .'

Gathering speed through suburbs flapping

with washing lines, and suddenly – the country! Fields, cows. Bye-bye, everyone, we're on our way.

Remember the little packet Maria stuffed in my pocket. Unwrapping it, gaze at a tiny framed photo of the two of us in the garden, me in Ireland's green, Maria in Brazilian blue and yellow, ball at our feet, deadliest duo on earth.

Sadie hanging out lapping air.

'Would you mind closing that window?'

It's Mrs Toad. Didn't hear a *please*, so we'll ignore it.

'There's an unholy draught, kindly close that window!'

Look her in the eye, do as I'm told. Sadie dumbly panting, nose to window. Place her dish on the floor – no, on the table! Fill it with mineral water and she's straight in – *slap-slap-slap* – her impossibly long tongue splashing the table. The Toad stares coldly. It's war.

Meanwhile, Little Toad's fiddling with something she doesn't want me to see. An inhaler! Join the club!

Big fat fly settles on the table. Zooms to investigate picnic smells, the delights lurking beneath tea towels.

'Oh, get away!' Mrs Toad flapping furiously.

Fly's too quick, keeps returning. Toad swats, fly flees and comes again, droning round her head.

'I ask you! First fleas, now flies.'

What! 'My dog doesn't have fleas.'

'All dogs have fleas, and I've a good mind . . .' looking up and down the carriage. 'My daughter has asthma. That animal should be in the guard's van!'

Fair enough, I'm thinking, and pull Sadie under the table.

'How far are you intending to travel?'

'Galway.'

'I might have guessed! Wait here,' she tells her daughter, and marches off down the train. Little Toad, lowering her eyes, takes a sly pull on her inhaler.

'You getting hungry?' I offer, meaning Sadie, but Little Toad looks up and says, 'Oh, no thanks!' and I'm starting to say, *I didn't mean you!* when I see she's gone red and flustered.

'What's her name?' asks Little Toad, glancing quickly over her shoulder.

'Sadie. She's never been further than Bray and I don't think she'll eat anything if I don't find her favourite snack – which isn't bull's brains or fillet of dinosaur, as you might imagine, but – got it!'

'Grapes!' Little Toad amazed.

Feeding one at time into snapping jaws. 'Mad for them, she is.'

Mrs Toad's back, without the Chief Inspector of Railways – just herself and a fixed smile. 'Come along, dear, pack everything up – they've found us superior accommodation.'

'Do you want a hand, carrying all that?' I offer.

'I'll think we'll manage, thank you. Goodbye!'

As she follows her ma, Little Toad gives me a little half smile, and I nod coolly in return. And feel bad. I could have been nicer.

As the Toads exit the carriage at one end, a ticket inspector enters from the other.

'Stay still, girl . . .' whipping out her blanket and covering her so not a hair is showing.

The inspector's getting nearer. Pull down bags and shove them in round Sadie. '*Shush*, or we're for it.'

The inspector's in the next cubicle, I'm breathing as quick as the train – *tum-tee-tum-tee-tum-tee-tum*. He's standing over me, clipping my ticket, leaning this way and that to look under the table. Sadie's paw's sticking out, and she's licking it.

'Is that your dog?'

No, it's the Pope's!

'It should be in the guard's van.'

'Please, mister, I'll keep her quiet.'

'You should have hired a box at Heuston Station.'

'I'd never put her in a box.'

'Sorry, son, I've had complaints.'

Lead Sadie like a condemned prisoner

through the train to the dreaded guard's van, a dim, rattling prison cell, empty but for a couple of bikes.

'You'll have to stay here with her now.'

'I wouldn't leave her for a minute.'

'Fair play to you,' he says and leaves.

Settle down on the floor with Sadie. 'We're going on an adventure –' stroking her big woolly head – 'a great big adventure . . .'

PART TWO

CONNEMARA, HERE I COME!

6

Galway's buzzing with heat, roads steaming after rain, sky washed blue. Follow Mum's idea, find nearby park, where Sadie picks a patch of grass to drown with pee, while I look for a bench to eat our sandwiches.

Run back to catch the Kilraine coach. In my grandparents' time you could take the train all the way, but the government ripped up the rails years ago. 'Vandalism of the worst kind!' says Mum.

Damn! The coach is full already. Tourist time.

'What now, Sadie, I don't fancy sleeping in the park.'

Another coach pulls up. Relief – till the driver sees Sadie. 'You're not intending bringing *that* on board?'

'That's an Irish wolfhound, with a distinguished pedigree.'

'Maybe so, but you and your pedigree will have to wait and see if there's room.'

'But I've got a ticket!'

'Does the hound have a ticket?'

Feel like kicking him up the backside.

Coach filling up, swallowing more and more people, driver looking round, happy as a hangman. 'Sorry, son, you'll have to get the next.'

'When's that?'

'Should be one more later on.'

'Should be?'

'Wait!' An elderly passenger banging the window. A seat at the back! Thanks! I wave.

Sadie riding the bumpy floor. Dust and bustle of Galway fading behind us. Here come craggy mountains and tumbling streams, boulders sticking up like giants' knees, wide empty lakes, solitary houses on distant shores, telegraph poles strung along the road like miles of washing lines, and everywhere sky – more sky than I've ever seen, different everywhere you look: here pink and blue, over there thunder-grey running to flaming orange and purple as the day winds down.

Heart beating, breath thinning – thought of meeting my wacky old aunt, and being stuck with her till Christmas.

Dark hills and church spires against the sky ahead – Kilraine! Modern buildings on the outskirts age rapidly towards the town centre; stone houses and hump bridges, wide main street. Pulling up with a sigh from the weary coach.

Sadie stretching with a wolfish yawn. Out into the air we tumble and – Where is she? No one to meet us, passengers melting away, cars vanishing into silence, we're left standing. Lights coming on. Air cold for May, fresh from the mountains. Lungs going, *Wow!* Sadie sitting down bewildered.

Stroking her, 'Don't worry, girl. If no one comes, we'll book into the best hotel, order saussies and fruit salad.'

Black hills against burning sky, clouds trailing like smoke. People piling into pub on corner, laughter evaporating. Cars going by, squint at drivers' faces, trying to remember what Dad's sister looks like.

High-pitched wailing, little old Citroën – tin can on wheels – tilting round the corner, shuddering to a stop. Out hops a woman in shabby raincoat and beret.

'Lorcan! Sadie! Will you ever forgive your Auntie Peig?' kissing my brow, patting weary Sadie. 'Were you waiting ages? I was waylaid by a neighbour looking for a lift, and then by a pair of brainless sheep in the middle of the road. Never mind all that, give me your bags. My! Look at you, you're nearly a man! Hop in – everyone's waiting to meet you!'

'Who's everyone? I thought you lived . . . ?'

'*Alone*? Heavens no!' zooming off with a deafening whine. 'There's Noel the crow – I found him at Christmas – Sally the goat

73

who eats my washing, and plenty more!'

'Who else?'

'Prudence the pig, Freddie the fearless pheasant, Nelson the one-eyed hedgehog, Ginger and Nutmeg – my two wretched cats – and Brandy, the dottiest sheepdog that ever lived.'

'Sounds wild!'

'And quite by chance, Lorcan. Began with a late neighbour's homeless donkey, and then a badger found tangled in wire, and an oil-drenched gull a little girl brought, and, with help from above, I do my best to heal them, and some stay and some prefer the wild – a movable feast, dear nephew; never a drab day.'

'What will Brandy say when he sees Sadie?'

'Here comes more misery to torment me!'

Like Peig already, and I've only known her five minutes!

Road climbing sharply out of town, up among giant boulders and overhanging trees, water darting under the road, shrubs sprouting from rocks – and then we're up above the twinkling lights of the town, climbing with the dark sea on one side, craggy slopes the other, and then the road stretches across a plain, empty as the first road, meandering between dry-stone walls and little fields in the fading light.

'It's so quiet.'

'Not a sinner on the road – only us!'

'Is it always this quiet?'

'Heavens no – you get three or four cars flying along in the rush hour.'

Miles of rolling green and rock – no concrete, office blocks or traffic lights. Road suddenly dipping and weaving as though alive, and look – the moon! Fine as a nail-cutting among the fir trees – and there! A flock of birds bursting from a tree, scattering like fish.

'Mind you, they're planning a dual carriage-way to run from Kilraine to Ballyconneely.'

'Is that good?'

'Oh yes . . . if you're one of those who hold that faster is always better, and that permanently disfiguring this unique land-scape is a fair price for knocking a few minutes off your journey.'

'You're not one of those then, Auntie?'

'I hope not. I'm supposed to be secretary of the Stop the Road campaign.'

'How do you propose to stop it?'

'I wish I knew, but they've given no hint where the road might go, leaving everyone on tenterhooks. Anyway, how's life in the fast lane?'

'Dublin? Bit mad now with all the traffic.'

'This'll be a switch. Rock, bog and deso-lation, that's what we're cursed with, and I love every stone! Weather's vile, roads potholes strung together, nights deep and lonesome –' *Bang!* Car hits hole and we all jump – 'See what I mean!' *Bang!* Another! 'But friends are plenty, the music's mighty and though we carp and grumble day and night, we wouldn't swap it for the world, sure we wouldn't.'

Whitewashed cottage ahead, thatched roof with tufts sticking up like it just got out of bed.

'Is that it, Auntie?'

'You like it?'

'Yes!'

'I'd have put in an offer, only it belongs to Gabriel Doon,' says Peig as we whiz by the house with its donkey and bicycle in the drive, 'and he might have something to say about it.'

Road rattles on towards the last chink of light, and I can just see by my watch it's – 'Twenty past ten?'

'That's about it.'

'And still a bit light.'

'Further west, honey.'

'Of course.'

Darkness falling fast, walls and fields closing in, Peig flicking on her lights and slowing to approach a bridge, bump over it and pick up speed along a road winking with ditches.

'About Gabriel – I should warn you, he looks a bit alarming. Problems with his birth. His

76

da did a runner and his ma died young. He's not much over twenty himself. He's one of my floating patients, you might say; spirits himself into the house. Problem with his speech, which doesn't help – sounds like a befuddled five-year-old. But he's all there in his way. Don't be afraid if you look up and he's sitting there. Here's our turning,' dropping down through the gears, throwing the car into a narrow lane.

Stony track lit by white rocks, headlights sweeping back and forth as if looking for the house – finding it hiding in trees and hedges.

'Home sweet home!'

Engine off – huge silence. Tumble out into air fizzing with insects and smelling of blossom. Light from the house through a gate marked SKYLARKS. Sadie sniffing round, disorientated, amazed. Peeing in the grass and sounding, in the silence, like Niagara Falls.

'You must be starving, hon.'

'Sadie, too, Auntie.'

'Soon fix that!'

Out come bags and cases, through a garden sweet with grass to a white, two-storey cottage. One lit window lively with moths.

'Lovely smell, Auntie.'

'Honeysuckle. Wonderful, isn't it?'

'That too, but I meant the smoke.'

'I thought you might like a fire.' Peig lifts the latch on a plain door, kicks it open.

'Don't you lock it, Auntie?'

Laughs, 'Where would I find the key?'

Squashed entrance hall, half-moon table and letter opener, hooks for coats, shelf for hats and a big torch.

'It's going to be such fun having you stay,' leading me through a low door. 'This is the drawing room.'

Wow! Big old room lost in time, shaggy turf fire humming in a fireplace deep enough to sleep in. An old piano – great!

'Make yourselves comfy. Brandy! Where are you? We have visitors!'

Sit at lacy table stroking Sadie, who's sticking close, wondering what we're doing here.

Clock ticking in the awful silence. Take in whitewashed walls and cubbyholes for books and trinkets, fireplace flanked by stacks of turf and logs, chipped piano with half-dead flowers on top, worn-out three-piece suite, uneven stone floor and rugs.

Whisper, 'Look, Sadie! Pussy cat. Two pussy cats.'

Scruffy little cat with chewed ears curled up in one armchair; sleek black cat in the other, watching us.

'Brandy must have gone calling,' Peig arriving with loaded tray.

'These the cats you were telling me about?'

'That scruffy little thing is Ginger, the mother, and Nutmeg, her beautiful son. Give

Ginger a wide birth for a bit. She's fiery as a box of bangers. Found her in the woodpile one freezing night. You've never seen a little scrap make itself so big to frighten me. Took weeks of titbits to coax her into the warm, and next morning at breakfast I counted six suckling kittens nearly as big as her. I kept one and look at him! The dad must have been a puma.'

'What happened to the other five?'

'I talked up their rat-catcher pedigree and found homes for the lot!'

Hot stew, thick bread and butter, mug of hot chocolate – all tasting *amazing*! Peig puts down a dish for Sadie, who approaches warily, sniffs, turns away.

'Come on, girl, give it a try.'

'Don't rush her, hon; it's all a bit strange.'

'What's in it, Auntie?'

'Same as yours, duck stew with pasta.'

'She wouldn't be used to fresh food.'

Peig sits opposite me sipping green tea. She's taken off her coat and beret and looks old – and young at the same time: eyes bright, wind-burned face wise with lines; long, shiny wolfhound-grey hair; jumper, skirt and boots – country woman.

Strange scratching noise!

'Go back to sleep, Noel!' Peig addressing someone in a cardboard box on a shelf. 'Meet him in the morning, hon. Broke a wing, don't ask me how. Joins me for breakfast, takes tea!'

Above the fireplace a curious photo: a couple and their two children, plus two men, one in cloth cap, the other a handsome fellow in army-style tunic, with long hair and beret.

'You and Dad as kids, Auntie?'

'Yes, nineteen sixty-five. And the feller in the beret – any guesses?'

'Um . . .' Don't want to sound too interested.

'Che Guevara!' says Auntie like a teacher with a particularly slow pupil.

'That his beret?' pointing to hers.

'I wish!'

'Why's everyone wearing his T-shirt?'

'Well, he was one of the greatest revolutionaries of our time. He also happened to be very handsome.'

'What did he do?'

'Didn't your father ever tell you?'

'I didn't really listen.'

'Then I'm sure you don't want me to bore you,' gazing at the photo, like she hasn't seen it for a while. 'Came to this very house,' she sighs, as if recalling a visit from Jesus.

'Why was he so great?'

'He wanted to change the world, no rich or poor, everyone equal. He began with the Caribbean island of Cuba, where rich Americans partied, but the average Cuban worked like a slave and died in poverty. Cuba was ruled by brutal dictator Fulgencio Batista. A young Cuban lawyer called Fidel

80

Castro had already led a doomed rebellion, and was flung out the country. Licking his wounds, Castro dreamed and schemed and set to sea in nineteen fifty-six with a hand-picked company of rebels, in a leaking boat called the *Grandma*.

'One of his men was a young Argentinian called Che Guevara. Che had just qualified as a doctor, but told his mother he was off to liberate the poor and oppressed of the world. It was a wild idea, a tiny force setting out to liberate a country run by a big army, but – as Che famously said to his nervous comrades – *Be realistic, pursue the impossible!*'

'He had asthma, didn't he?'

'Yes! Too sick to go to school as a child; his mama taught him at home. They even moved house to get away from the river.'

'So they sailed to Cuba?'

'Rough seas swept them onto the wrong part of the island. Batista's men fell upon them, killed most of them. Hiding in the jungle with a handful of survivors, Che – chief medical officer – found himself carrying two backpacks, one containing medical supplies, the other ammunition. *Which will I throw away?* he asked himself. He discarded the medicine and became a guerrilla leader.'

'Did Batista go after them?'

'You bet! Hunted on the ground, bombed from the air, they escaped to the hills of the

Sierra Maestra and rallied the peasants into a guerrilla army. The peasants loved Che. As well as training them and tending their wounds, he found time to teach them to read and write. The rebels hit back, and little by little fought Batista's army to a standstill.'

Sadie's starting to eat – thank God. But who's that? Somebody growling, and it isn't Sadie.

'It's all right, Brandy –' Peig clicking fingers – 'we've got visitors.' Poking through the bead curtain, a slender sheepdog, teeth bared, eyes fixed on Sadie. Sadie curls her lip, lets out a low growl.

'She doesn't usually do that,' reaching for Sadie's collar.

'Brandy, come meet Cousin Sadie.'

Brandy remaining crouched, growling.

'*Here!*' goes Peig. Instant obedience. 'Sit. Good girl. Sadie better sleep upstairs with you for now, hon.'

'Did Che Guevara fight too, with his asthma?'

'Oh yes, he was a brave fighter. But sometimes he couldn't breathe and had to be stretchered through the jungle by his men. But his energy was legendary. Even as a top minister in the new government, he worked with the volunteer brigades in the sugarcane fields and construction sites, never stopping to rest until they begged him, *Che, for pity's sake, we're all pooped!'*

'What was he doing in Connemara, Auntie – in your house?'

'Engine trouble stranded him at Shannon airport on his way back to Cuba from some diplomatic mission, and he thought he'd check out his roots – because, you know, his dad's name was Ernesto Guevara *Lynch*; his ancestors included Irish aristocrats.'

'Are we related to Che Guevara, Auntie?'

'Only vaguely.'

'Like ghostly cousins?'

'Why not! So he hopped in a taxi and went for a spin, and was so captivated he kept going, until he spotted a young girl and her little brother by the side of the road and stopped to talk to us.'

'You and Dad?'

'We gazed up at this tall foreigner with the laughing eyes. Never seen anyone like him. Your grandad appeared, invited him in. And so Che Guevara stepped across this hearth and kissed my mother's hand.'

'That the cab driver in the photo?'

'That's him. We sat down to dinner, and gradually the identity of our guest emerged. My parents' jaws nearly hit the floor. The most famous revolutionary in the world was sitting at our table! They couldn't have been more astonished if the Pope himself had dropped by. Well! Word went out, cousins and neighbours arrived with fiddles and tin whistles, and it was a rare and wonderful evening! And since it was too late and stormy to return to the airport, the cabbie stretched out on the couch, and your dad and I made way for our honoured guest. Che refused, of course. He would have slept on the woodpile! But our parents insisted, and Che slept four hours in the bed that's now yours, and was gone before dawn.'

A shiver goes through me.

My bedroom's small, with faded wallpaper and sloping ceiling, wooden beam you have to duck under, crooked floor that creaks, ancient wardrobe, little desk and chair in a small, deep-set window looking out on the front garden and faraway lights of Kilraine. I've a bedside table and lamp, dish of lavender and an empty drawer. Big double bed with iron frame, facing a fireplace with sprays of dried flowers. Clock on mantelpiece says ten to midnight. Above hangs a painting of a pony and trap on an empty road, signed P. LYNCH. Peig, I suppose.

Curling up in the same bed Che Guevara once slept in. I can almost feel him in the room, watching me. Clock ticking in the awful silence.

'All right, Sadie?'

No reply. Lean over and she's lying on an old blanket on the floor, head on paws, eyes shining in faint light from the window.

'It'll be fine, Sadie, you'll see.'

I can't sleep if she can't.

Loud ringing downstairs! Old-fashioned phone – sit up, heart beating. Peig saying, 'Oh hello! . . . Not at all, I'm still up – nice to hear you. How's Bonn? . . . He's splendid, a great boy . . . Yes, good journey on the whole, except I was late meeting him. Shall I wake him?'

Out of bed, halfway to the door.

'You sure? . . . I'll tell him. Bye, Maggie, God bless.'

Wait! Too late. Creep back under the covers thinking of Mum in her hotel bed, Dad in his rotten cell, Gerry asleep at home. Listening to the silence, disturbed now and then by a faraway car, somebody going somewhere. Turn on my side, thinking of the new school I've to face on Monday. Thank God tomorrow's Sunday . . .

Something pressing on my feet wakes me: Sadie sprawled across the bed. Curtains moving in the window, horse and trap over the mantelpiece still plodding along the lonely lane. All's quiet, just Sadie noisily licking herself, a bee droning in a madly flowering window box. Eyes all crackly – must have slept like the dead.

A cock crowing, loud as a car alarm. I'm in the country!

Prop photo of me and Maria on the mantelpiece and look out the window – the shock of the view! Hugeness of light and space, higgledy-piggledy fields, empty roads, distant slopes dotted with sheep, faraway houses scattered like pebbles beneath craggy peaks, and everything veiled in mist. Below, the front garden a virtual meadow humming with insects.

Heart beating. So used to streets and houses, roads fuming with cars, buses, sirens, dust and glass, and here – miles and miles of rolling hush.

Open a suitcase, throw on some clothes.

'Come on, girl, gently now.'

Venture onto the landing. From the bathroom window look out the back at a sprawling, trampled garden loosely fenced. Peig hanging washing on a line looped between flowering trees. Frisky white goat – Sally? – nibbling her skirt. Hens wandering about scratching the ground, among them a limping black pig – Prudence? – wiggling her snout. One hen has a crowd of chicks darting here and there like wind-up toys, crowding round her beak to see what she's found.

Over to one side an open barn sheltering bales of hay, garden tools, a cultivator, big woodpile and turf stack.

Unzip wash bag, lay out my things next to Peig's. It's a basic bathroom, peeling walls, plank floor, antique bath with brass taps.

Sadie sticking to me going down. No sign of Brandy, Ginger or Nutmeg. Through a bead curtain into the kitchen – *Woh!* On the draining board is a big black thing with awesome beak, staring haughtily, like, *Who do you think you are?* One of his wings drooping.

'That's Noel the crow, Sadie. I wouldn't go too close. Let's look outside.'

'Good morning, children! How did you sleep?' Peig shyly kissing me, ruffling Sadie's head.

Sadie looking around, tilting her head. Madhouse! Hens scratching, chicks whizzing by, Sally the goat, startled, leaping onto the turf stack; and here comes Prudence the pig to give Sadie a good sniff, looking her over as if to say, *Hmm, interesting!* and limping away again.

Angry growling! Dog creeping along a low wall.

'Don't be silly, Brandy!' says Peig. 'Come here – *here*! And you too, Sadie, sit – *sit*!'

Sadie sits! Amazing.

'Brandy, say good morning to your cousin Sadie from Dublin. You're living together now, and the sooner you get used to it the better!'

Day flies by. Wish I could slow it down. Peig does her best to distract me, kits me out with wellies and rain jacket and away we go, through a ramshackle vegetable garden and up a hill to a jagged dry-stone wall marking the boundary of her property, Brandy and Sadie trotting along ignoring each other. A stone stile breaches the wall: we're in open country, damp, lush and sparkling.

A donkey! Golden-brown woolly thing, crying urgently, *Hee-hor, hee-hor!* 'What's wrong with it, Auntie?'

'That's Buttons, Gabriel's lovesick donkey, calling to his mate and foal below. See them?'

'Yes!'

'She's called Sunshine, and her foal's called Hiccups.'

Buttons stops to watch us climb a stile and start down a squishy track towards the sea when suddenly – 'Where's Sadie?' No sign of her. Oh no! She's wandered off and broken a leg! Lying in pain somewhere, crows pecking her eyes out!

'Brandy, find Sadie!' says Peig. 'Quick!'

Brandy hesitates – *Oh, all right then!* – and trots back the way we've come, and there's Sadie! Waiting patiently on the far side of the stile, stuck!

'Silly Lorcan – leaving you on your own!'

Help her over and on we go, till Peig stops. 'Shh, I wanted to show you the holy well, but Gabriel's there. I thought he was out on his boat. We'll not disturb him.'

Can just make out a man and his bicycle among the trees.

'What's he doing?'

'Sips the water and leaves little offerings.'

'Like what?'

'Seashells, empty baked bean tins.'

The figure's doing a dance, playing a tin whistle.

Drizzly rain, salty on the lips. Return to Skylarks – which isn't white at all; it's soft, faded pink. Brass plaque by the front door reads: DR P LYNCH, CONSULTANT ACUPUNCTURIST, with loads of letters to show how qualified she is.

'Where's your practice, Auntie?'

'Right here,' opening a hall door.

'Mind if I . . .?'

'Work away.'

I wander into a cramped but modern reception area with couch and magazines, shelves crammed with herbal teas and sleeping tablets, sunflower seeds and soya milk. Two curtained-off cubicles, each furnished with bed, chair and electric heater. On a wall a framed poster—

> If all the medications in the world
> Were thrown in the sea
> It'd be a great day for mankind
> But a bad one for the fish!
>
> *Thomas Edison*

'You've got a PC, Auntie!'

'It's getting old. Time I upgraded it.'

Maybe I can e-mail Gerry after all.

'Feel free, honey,' says Peig, reading my thoughts; 'long as you don't delete my patients' records.'

Sun going down, breathing getting thinner. Hadley Wood uniform laid out ready for tomorrow. Peig didn't get enough warning to buy me Raven Hill's.

The men of 1815 facing each other across the bedroom floor, rubber bands wreaking havoc, murderous cannonades drowning out the cries of— Phone ringing below! Heart leaps! But no, it's not Mum.

The dice are cruel, Napoleon's forces in tatters –

'Take that, you impertinent French froggies—'

Phone again! Heart stops.

'Lorcan, hon, it's for you!'

Historically dodgy phone call halts Waterloo.

'Ma, you've done it again!'

'What?'

'Interrupted history!'

Early to bed. 'Night-night, honey! Night-night, Sadie!'

'Night-night, Auntie.'

Lights out, wide awake. Look out the window. Sadie hopping up to join me, paws on sill. *Wow!* Nearly blinded! 'Look at that . . .'

Sky's black velvet and huge with stars, millions of them, great fistfuls of glitter.

8

Doomsday – wind shaking the trees, rain lashing my window. Last night was all so still and starry!

Tying my Hadley tie – could easily fool myself I'll be seeing Gerry, Miss Hart and Mr Lucky.

'Sadie, you got to stay with Peig and Brandy today.'

Downstairs, Peig on one knee on the back step feeding – a hedgehog! One good eye and a wrinkly smudge where the other should be.

'Morning, kids. Meet Nelson – very partial to scrambled egg.'

'How did he lose the eye?'

'Who knows? Difference of opinion with a fox?'

Peig puts down dish for Sadie, breakfast on the table for me – eggs, bacon and saussies, crusty white toast and brown soda bread, jars of home-made marmalades and jams,

Connemara honey, pot of tea under knitted cosy, jug of orange juice . . .

'Enough there for you, hon?'

'Just about!'

She won't be taking me to school, she has patients all morning.

'Here's your packed lunch. Remember where to get the bus? Go straight to the Head Teacher and I'll pick you up at three forty-five. Have a ball! And Lorcan . . .'

'Yes?'

'Anyone gives you trouble, look him in the eye and think of Che Guevara!'

Standing at rain-swept crossroads, surrounded by rock and fields and grass bending in the wind, which comes in gusts, stops for a breather and gusts again, punching my umbrella inside out. Odd car flies by, road empty again. Miles of rolling cloud, a solitary white horse watching me over a wall.

Here comes something – a white coach, filling the air with noise, yet still way off, swaying with the road, slowing as the driver sees my hand, slowing and . . . roaring on! Driver peering out as if to say, *I don't pick up the likes of you.*

'Hey!' running. *'Hey!'*

Coach staggering to a stop. 'Don't think you want this one, son,' says the driver.

Gasping, 'Raven Hill? Only uniform I got.'

'Ah, in that case . . .'

Everyone staring, boys and girls. I forgot it was mixed. Two pairs of empty seats. Sit alone gazing out at purple fields and rain. Someone passing snide remarks. I must be the only kid in Connemara with a flaming brolly. Must look a right eejit. Bet Che Guevara never carried one. Was hoping their uniform would be navy like mine, but it's maroon and grey, sweatshirt instead of my blazer. No one speaks to me. Why would they?

Bus slowing, passing a travellers' halting site: mobile homes, washing lines, dogs and kids, heaps of scrap metal. Red-haired boy by side of road wearing the maroon and grey, blank face and earring. Gets on without looking at anyone, goes for the remaining pair of empty seats.

Crawling through somewhere called Ballinscar, pupils collecting in the rain, and a sign – RAVEN HILL COMMUNITY SCHOOL. Not the cottage school I expected – big, sprawling site, shockingly modern against the surrounding rock and hills.

Get off with everyone else and trail along with my shameful umbrella rolled up. I'd accidentally lose it, but it's not mine. Stuff it wet into my school bag. How's the breathing? Could be worse. Stay cool – you're doing fine.

Some kids pushing in are mere smidgens; others look bigger than the teachers climbing out of cars. What do they feed them on? And look! That plump girl up ahead, isn't that . . . ? What was her name? On the train with her ma who hated Sadie – *Little Toad!* I'm not alone, I know someone! Speed up to catch her – and lose her in the crush.

Bell's ringing – not the old *ting-a-ling* that used to shoo us along in Hadley Wood; a deafening *DOO-DOO-DOO-DOO* like an alarm in a nuclear power plant. Kids barging by in all directions, teachers calling, 'Move along! Skates on!'

Left standing in foyer with trophies, potted plants, Jesus peering down from his cross, sad eyes looking into mine saying, *See what happens to outcasts like you and me*.

Door marked STAFF ROOM; another says OFFICE.

Inhaler to lips, quick pull – *Knock-knock*.

'Come in.'

Fussy-looking secretary frowning at my uniform.

'I'm Lorcan Lynch, and—'

'Ah, the boy from Dublin,' she says, like I've landed from Mars. 'With the, um, famous father.'

Think she means infamous – her phone's ringing, she's pointing me to a door marked MR P. W. TRENCH, HEAD.

Knock-knock.

'Yes!' comes a cheery voice.

95

In we go, and there's Mr Trench, working a PC at a wide desk. He's a rosy-cheeked, roundy-faced man with baldy head. Kindly eyes peering at me over specs: 'Ah, would you by any chance be . . . ?'

'Lorcan Lynch.'

'The man himself! Delighted! All the way from Dublin. Mystery man to boot, except to expect asthma fits. Would these be a common occurrence?'

'Not the really bad ones.'

'How do you define really bad?'

'Ones that require hospital . . . two or three a year.'

'And the others?'

'Once or twice a month. I can manage them, with a bit of oxygen.'

'I've already alerted Dr Sweeney and arranged for oxygen.'

'Thank you, sir.'

'Any problems, let Miss Maddigan know. She'll take good care of you. Otherwise, we'll expect the best, will we not! Infirmities, I always say, should never be an excuse for under-achievement or poor conduct, don't you agree?'

'I never take advantage, sir. In fact, I don't see it as a infirmity any more.'

'Really?'

'It can make you stronger. More determined.'

'Excellent fellow!' he goes. 'But tell me, are

you planning to sport that alien attire round my school?'

'My aunt didn't get enough warning to buy the Raven Hill uniform.'

'I'll have my secretary lend you something until your aunt can at least purchase the correct sweatshirt.'

Rising to show me out, 'Report to room nine, work hard and keep out of trouble. Raven Hill revels in its reputation for well-behaved, high-achieving pupils. Understand?'

'Yes, sir.'

'Good. Enjoy your stay.'

Feel the heat of his eyes on my back, branding me 'trouble'. I hate this place already, these empty echoing corridors, numbered doors – 3, 4, 5; breath getting thinner and faster – 7, 8 – glimpses of girls and boys at desks – 9.

MISS MADDIGAN.

Quick blast on trusty inhaler, hands sweaty on doorknob – *Knock-knock*.

'Yessssss!' comes a merry shout.

Enter lions' den – everyone staring, including Miss Maddigan, tall with pale, pinched face and spiky hair dyed a reddy colour, like a funny witch.

'Just a moment' – returning to the board, leaving me standing in the glare of a thousand eyes. Meet them head on – nice and easy.

'Mr Lynch, I presume!' Miss Maddigan

beaming. 'You're very welcome. Make yourself at home beside TJ; we'll chat in a minute.'

Unpack a few pens, look relaxed, check the breathing, glance up and catch the eye of a dark-haired girl and smile. She keeps looking – freckly face, eyes there's no escape from, sizing me up. Funny feeling I'm looking at a friend – or mortal enemy.

Same for my neighbour TJ, who has T. J. DE BARRA printed on his pencil box and gives off dangerous vibes and still hasn't acknowledged me – not a look or a whisper. Sideways glance reveals handsome fellow with blond, wavy hair. Feels me looking and turns his head slowly. I smile. He doesn't.

Look away, cool as a cat, beating inside – and suddenly realize – T. J. *de Barra*, the name of the boss of Galaxy Holdings, Dad's enemy, who wanted him jailed and owns an island down here. Is TJ related? Must be, with a name like that.

Glance about: there's that red-haired traveller boy sitting alone, wrapped in his own world, rings on his fingers. And there's Little Toad at the front, getting on with her work.

Miss Maddigan's calling me. Leave my place and feel all the eyes following me, the ears twitching as I answer questions like, *How was your journey?* and *Where are you staying?* and . . . 'Any hobbies, dear?'

Mind blank – 'Um . . . piano, cricket,

98

re-enactments of the Battle of Waterloo with toy soldiers.'

Sniggers from the back.

'How interesting. And what subjects do you like?'

'Everything, all subjects.'

Muffled jeers from same boy.

'Thank you, Clinton, that'll do!' Softly again, 'How would you like to give a five-minute talk? Everybody's doing one. Choose your own subject, use the board, bring in pictures. Most boys have picked a favourite team, girls a favourite band. On the other hand, TJ de Barra gave a riveting account of fishing on Inishbán.'

Cheers from TJ's many fans. Inishbán – the White Island – could that be the one his father owns?

'And Róisín Kennedy enthralled us with the life cycle of the pipistrelle bat –' groans of boredom – 'which I for one thoroughly enjoyed.' Miss Maddigan smiles at Little Toad's bowed head. 'And Blaise McBride has chosen Countess Markiewicz –' even louder groans – 'which I'm really looking forward to.'

Everyone looking at the dark-haired, freckly girl.

'We'll need earplugs, miss,' says TJ.

'Road builders' earmuffs!' calls Clinton.

'Mind your manners! Now you understand, Lorcan, why I have to keep those two apart.'

'Seriously, miss,' says TJ, 'Blaise and her talks do my head in.'

Blaise gives a contemptuous snort and carries on reading.

'You could talk about Dublin, dear. Most of these simple souls have never strayed outside the county, and could benefit from a bit of culture.'

'Who cares about Dublin?' cries Clinton, who's too big for his desk, too big for his schoolboy voice. 'Not a patch on Galway.'

'The Abbey Theatre, the Gate, the Peacock . . . *ah*!' sighs Miss Maddigan. 'Alphabetically speaking, Lorcan, you happen to be next! Unless we can switch you with –' checking the list – 'Miss McBride?'

Blaise lifts her eyes from her work and shrugs. All the same to her.

'That's settled then. Blaise Wednesday, Lorcan Friday. I'm not rushing you?'

'Friday's fine,' says I, cursing myself. Are you nuts? *Friday?* Why not offer to give a lecture on astrophysics while you're at it!

TJ ignoring me all morning. Actually he doesn't. Keeps murmuring things like, 'You're sitting in Clint's place,' and 'Stuff Dublin!' to which I reply, 'Wasn't my idea – nor was Dublin.'

Dark-haired Miss Freckles – What was her name? Blaise? – has her head buried in her books. The traveller boy hasn't spoken to a soul, sits chewing a pencil, gazing out the window. Little Toad – or Róisín Kennedy – looks just as isolated and twice as miserable, taking occasional pulls on her inhaler. Observing them, I see that the traveller boy seems content on his own, whereas Little Toad looks desperate. Lovely name, *Ro-sheen*, 'Little Rose', for such a sad case.

Break time. Too wet to go out; sit at my desk reading, talking to no one, noticing how TJ and Clinton, playing games on their mobiles, give weaker kids a hard time:

'Stop squeaking, Toe-rag!' they taunt a little boy with hedgehog haircut. 'You're blocking the light, Fatty!' they tell Little Toad. They push people around in a casual, lazy way, and no one objects – not a word. Everyone's frightened of them, except the traveller boy, who acts invisible and untouchable, communicating with no one, and no one with him.

Back to work. Maths with Mr Oates, who stoops and turns his head very slowly like a tortoise. Peering over half-moon spectacles, he's calling pupils out to stand representing geometrical shapes, and now he's signalling me, and I'm out front with TJ and the traveller, switching from being a right-angled triangle to an isosceles triangle, an equilateral to an obtuse. I know all this, and the traveller learns fast, but TJ can't be fagged, slouches round, hands in pockets, too cool for triangles.

Back in our places, TJ whispering, 'You trying to show me up?'

Look him in the eye. 'You did that yourself.'

Gives me a look which says, *I'm gonna have to deal with you*.

Rain's stopped. Wander out at lunch time to eat sandwiches on a low wall, rocky hills and open sky for company, and a glittering dragonfly pausing at my elbow for a sunbath, monstrous yellow thing thick as a finger. An omen? A warning?

Little Toad takes a pull on her inhaler and wanders nearer and nearer, hoping I'll notice. The dragonfly darts away into the blue.

'Don't you remember me?' Little Toad shielding her eyes. 'The train. Your dog splashed everywhere and gobbled grapes. I'm Róisín.'

'Lorcan.'

'I know.'

'What were doing in Dublin, Róisín?'

Breathless: 'My cousin's wedding. Married a Romanian called Doro who works in a pizza restaurant. Mam wasn't too happy, but he's real sweet and brung me a traditional doll from Romania, not that I like dolls – me, I like astronomy and Westlife – meteorites, eclipses, phases of the moon. Do you like Westlife?'

'Not much.'

102

'Taking pictures?'

'Not really.'

'Oh.'

I sit on the wall, she stands beside it, neither knowing what to say. See the traveller boy flinging a tennis ball against a wall. 'Who's that, Róisín?'

'Joseph Tully. Sticky Joe. He's a knacker, keeps himself to himself.'

Her choice of language shocks me. Calling a traveller boy knacker is like calling a black kid nigger. If I referred to 'knackers' at home, Mum would go mad.

'Knacker's not a nice word,' says I.

Little Toad looks startled, blushes, like no one's pulled her up before, like it's normal here calling a fellow pupil knacker behind his back.

'And why Sticky?'

'When he first came, he carried a stick, and when teacher confiscated it, he always had a couple more in his bag, ready to whack anyone who came near.'

'How does he get on with TJ and Clinton?'

'He had a fight with Clinton first day, bloodied each other up about equal. Then TJ and Clinton started ganging up, and Sticky keeps well away. Only thing to do.'

'What about Blaise McBride?'

'*Blaise!*' sniffing in disgust. 'Weird! I mean real weird.'

'Like how, weird?'

'Mad on animals – *meat's murder* and *hunting's terrorism!* She's got a police record!'

'What for?'

'Threw a brick through the new McDonald's in Kilraine.'

I look up and there's Blaise reading a book against a wall. Knows who we're talking about.

All at once – surrounded! Gang of boys from my class with lively musical accents: 'Is Dublin real cool, like, Lorcan?'

'I suppose.'

'What school were you at?'

'It was called Hadley Wood. All boys.'

'Was it real posh?'

'You had to wear suits and dickie bows.'

'Never!'

'D'ye play Gaelic?' They're talking about Gaelic football, a manic mix of soccer and rugby, which I've never played.

'No, but I'd really like to.'

'We'll teach ye – d'you like Man United?'

'Not especially.'

'Who d'you support then?'

'Liverpool, Juventus, Ireland and Brazil.'

Looking at me funny. You're not supposed to give a list.

'I'm Thomas,' pipes little boy with hedgehog haircut, the one they called Toe-rag. 'You wanna steer clear of them two.'

Look up and meet the eyes of TJ and Clinton, leaning on a wall, planning their move against me. Feel like a rabbit in the open, hawks circling overhead. Laughing, 'You think I'm afraid of them?'

Audience squinting at me: *Either this feller's cool, or a complete eejit.*

'Their das are big round here too.'

'Yeah, TJ's da's the biggest poverty developer in Galway!' says Hedgehog Thomas.

'In Ireland, eejit! And it's *property*, not poverty.'

'And Clinton's da is Willie-John McNulty, our TD. Whatever they say round here goes . . . you listening?'

So TJ *is* Jack de Barra's son, and Clinton is the son of another of Dad's enemies. Dying for a blast on the inhaler, but not in front of this lot.

Rescued by the buzzer, boys drifting away and I follow, joined all at once by a cluster of giggling girls walking me into class—

'I'm Majella, and this is my friend Denise.'

'Yeah, and I'm Courtney, so watch it!' warns a tall, blue-eyed girl pointing a finger at me, all under the gaze of TJ and Clinton. Only Blaise McBride remains aloof, like a banished queen.

Afternoon drags. Gaze out the window. Then – *I know that car!* Peig's little Citroën arriving like a banshee, mixing it with the big cars at the gate.

Doo-doo-doo-doo, buzzer goes! I'm nearly out the window.

'Hop in, hon! How was your first day?'

Sadie and Brandy in the back. Sadie clambering over to lick me.

'Brilliant, Auntie! Real nice teachers.'

'The kids all right with you?'

'Yep, mostly.'

Bouncing and wailing down windy roads. Glancing at me, 'Someone give you trouble?'

'Not really, only I've to prepare a talk by Friday.'

'Friday – sure, you've plenty of time.'

'On Dublin or – wolfhounds! I could bring Sadie in.'

'Well, I've a grand little library, or you can go on line, long as you don't—'

'Delete your patients' records! Or Liverpool, or Juventus. That's what most of the boys are doing.'

'You want to be like them?'

'Don't we all want to fit in with everyone else?'

'Depends if you want to be a leader or a follower.'

'You sound like my dad, Auntie.'

'*Ha!*' she laughs. 'He was always a tearaway, your dad. Aged six he'd rather starve than submit to an injustice.'

'What am I, do you think, Auntie – leader or follower?'

'Interesting. A follower, I'd say – with the makings of a leader.'

'How do you mean?'

'Well, God gifts us with free choice. We're free to decide whether to run with the crowd, or try and lead the crowd in new directions.'

Driving in thoughtful silence.

'There's a girl called Blaise giving a talk on Countess Markiewicz.'

'That'll be interesting. Why not give yours on Che Guevara? The day he came to Connemara. Visited *our* house?'

'They won't know who he is.'

'Educate them!'

Wild! Running with Sadie, wind in our hair
and feet squelching, climbing the hill above
Peig's property and suddenly – the Atlantic!
Miles of foamy ocean, breakers rolling in from
America. And way over there, in the estuary,
an island with a big old house and white cliffs.
Is that it – Inishbán?

Don't want to think about TJ and Clinton,
or Friday's talk. Run back, polish off homework and dig out Dad's soldiers. Soon the air's
hot with grapeshot, thunder of cavalry and
Napoleon crying, 'You Eengleesh roz beefs, I
will kick your bottoms all ze way home to
Dovair!' – and Wellington mumbling, 'Damn,
blast and bleddy hell, where are those perish-
ing Prussians they promised?'

Strange noise in the front garden, like an
angry rubber duck. Look out and spy a beautiful bird in the grass, with painted face and
long trailing tail feathers. 'Look, Sadie – a
pheasant. Magnificent, isn't he?'

Peig appears below. 'Hello, stranger; been courting again, you bold bird? Get back, Brandy! You'll scare him.'

'What you feeding him, Auntie?'

'Currant buns, hon. Mad for them.'

Pheasant jumps back at my voice.

'It's all right, Freddie, Lorcan's family. I'm off to the shop, hon. I left Che Guevara on the PC, if you're interested. Come on, Brandy.'

Peig's engine dies away, sun slants into my room, setting light to the blood-soaked battle-field, where Napoleon has just been blown clean off his horse. 'Oooh-la-la, *ze empereur* is—'

Noises! Downstairs this time. Someone moving about very quietly – Noel the crow? No, too loud. Burglar? Wish I'd brought my cricket bat.

Creeping down, Sadie on my heels. Enter drawing room – no crow, only Ginger asleep in a chair – but I've a feeling someone was here just now. Carefully peering through bead curtain into kitchen. Back door wide open. Hens scratching among the weeds, Prudence the pig dozing in the mud, Sally the goat reclining on the turf pile, dreamily chewing. Sadie sniffs around, approaches the pig, tail wagging.

'Careful, Sadie.'

It's OK. Pig doesn't mind being sniffed.

Return indoors, into Peig's practice. It's

him, staring back at me from the screen – Che Guevara, man of destiny. Not in the mood for men of destiny, wander back to gloomy drawing room, where evening's arrived and everything's in shadow. Sit at the rickety piano, pick out a few keys and sing,

> *'You may be kings of Raven Hill*
> *Making everybody obey your will*
> *But let me tell you everyone*
> *I'm just a rabbit who refuses to run*
> *I'm just a rabbit who—'*

Whoops, I'm not alone. Someone's in the room, watching me. Hear his breath, feel his eyes on my neck. Turn slowly – *Holy smoke!* Someone sitting there with screwy eyes and bristly chin and teeth sticking out – Quasimodo's brother staring at me open-mouthed, skin and bones in a scarecrow's jacket, boils on his nose and wispy hair. Whips out a tin whistle and starts playing.

'Hello.' My voice!

Stops playing, stares. The bundle of fur in his lap stretches, *miaows* and settles again.

'I'm Lorcan, Peig's nephew.'

Swallows, stares.

'Are you Gabriel?'

'Me Gable – yis!'

'Pleased to meet you.'

'Please meety you – soggy.'

110

'Soggy?'

'Soggy – yis.'

'Oh, sorry – why?'

'Gable hard t'understand, cozzy peach feck.'

'Speech defect? I understand you perfectly.'

'Oh.' Blows a couple more spitty notes on his whistle, strokes the cat.

'You like Ginger, Gabriel?'

Crooked smile. 'Gable like all Goddy craters – yis!'

'Just wait till you meet Sadie!'

Sadie hears me, lopes in, stops dead.

'Sadie, meet Gabriel.'

'Ooh!' Gabriel's eyes pop. 'Wolf!'

'Wolf*hound*. Big softie.'

'Pig shoftie' – rigid, as Sadie approaches sniffing.

'It's OK, Gabriel, she's very gentle.'

Ginger opening her eyes, spiking up – *hissssss!*

Phone ringing makes me jump. 'Do you think we should get that, Gabriel?'

Gabriel looks startled.

'Maybe better leave it,' I'm thinking aloud. But then, what if it's . . . ?

Hop up and lift chunky old receiver.

'Hello? Peig Lynch's residence . . . Sorry? Ma! It's me! . . . How's it going? Are you giving them hell? . . . I'm fine – school's cool . . . Peig's place is wild! Animals everywhere and you can see for miles and the sky last night,

111

Ma, you've never seen so many stars in all your life. Is Dad OK?'

Cool and grey, clouds pressing down on hills and fields, soaking my lungs, making me snatch breath running for the bus in my borrowed Raven Hill sweatshirt, meeting all those eyes and some spark saying, 'Where's yer brolly, Olly?'

Where's yer brain? I was going to reply, but it's not worth it. Sit alone, look out at scraggy fields and crooked walls, ghost horses grazing in the mist.

There's Sticky Joe, hands in pockets by the side of the road, red hair black with rain. Boards without a word, lean-limbed and mean-looking – like, *Don't touch me, I'm dangerous!* Looking for a pair of empty seats, but there isn't one. He'll have to sit with someone. Hope it's me, but he drops into the nearest seat, travels with arms folded, looking straight ahead.

Miss Maddigan complaining of migraine, pops pills, makes us work in silence. Time drags, damp air finds its way in, tickles my lungs, makes me wheeze. TJ whispering, 'What's wrong – smoking too many Marlboros?'

Look him in the eye. 'Sixty a day.'

Looks daggers at me. Doesn't like my cheek, or anything about me.

Break time at last, everyone straining
get out. Little Toad and Hedgehog Thom
swapping Westlife gossip, walking too slow
for some people's liking.

'Move it, Toe-rag,' TJ brushing Thomas
aside.

'And you, Fatso,' Clinton barging by.

Little Toad and Thomas hop obediently out
the way. Little Toad even goes, 'Oh, sorry!'
And it all happens in front of me, as if to say,
*This is how it goes round here, new boy, so
what you gonna do about it?*

Shouldn't I say something? Do something?
No, you'll only get in trouble.

On the other hand ... Yes! You should
intervene, otherwise you're – What's Dad
always say? Colluding? If you don't stand up
and say something when evil's going on, then
you might as well be in on it. You're either
with evil, or against it.

Quick! Say something, before it's too late. 'I
think her name's Róisín!' Hell, I've said it!
'And his, if I recall, is Thomas!'

TJ and Clinton stop, turn, meet my gaze.

Shaking inside; outside cool as rain.
Thomas and Little Toad looking on, mortified.
TJ and Clinton exchange looks, like, *Right,
that's it!* and walk on, whispering.

Follow breezily into playground.

Sky's breaking up, air cool and sweet, and
my breathing curiously steady, considering

I've just thrown down a challenge to the school tyrants. Sit on my wall thinking how weird it is being here: no Gerry, Miss Hart or Mr Lucky. All this wilderness and sky. Boys chasing footballs, girls collecting in noisy huddles, monstrous seagulls wheeling overhead like eagles looking for fat little first years to feed their young.

Thinking of Mum stalking government ministers abroad, Dad doing press-ups in his cell, Maria tidying the empty house, when all at once I'm not alone – TJ and Clinton hopping up to sit either side of me, TJ relaxed, Clinton kind of smirking, like he's looking forward to a bit of gore. Supposed to be scared, and I am.

Waiting for them to say something, but TJ examines his nails like a movie gangster, and Clinton whistles lazily as he unwraps a sweet and pops it in his gob. Trying to scare me even more, and it's working.

TJ looking at me – 'Naff name.'

'What?'

'Lorcan's a naff name.'

'No it's not.'

'A nerd's name,' says Clinton. 'Nerdiest I ever heard.'

'Then you haven't heard your own.'

TJ and Clinton lean forward to exchange a lethal look.

'D'you hear that, Boss?' says Clinton. 'Only

here two wet minutes and disrespecting us already.'

'What did you have to pick this place for?' says TJ.

'I like the view.'

'This school, eejit.'

'For a laugh, what else?'

'Or because your dad's banged up, right?'

'Leave my dad out of it.'

'You're Jailchick from now on,' TJ informs me.

'Son of Jailbird – get it?' explains Clinton.

Easy shrug. 'Call me what you like, but you're peeing into the wind, because I only answer to Lorcan.'

'Stuff Lorcan,' says TJ. 'We're renaming you Jailchick Lynch. How d'you like that?'

'You two make me laugh, you really do.'

TJ shaking his head sadly, 'Doesn't get it, does he, Clint?'

'Better give him the rules,' Clinton agrees, popping another sweet, letting the breeze take the wrapper.

Blowing away across the playground, the sweet wrapper finds Sticky Joe watching from a distance.

'There's rules for new boys,' says TJ. 'Rule One is that you will, at all times, address me as Boss. That clear?'

'You want me to call you Boss?'

'Rule Two,' says Clinton, leaning in close, so

I get a good view of fillings and scraps of toffee in his teeth, 'you will at all times address me as *Mr* McNulty.'

'Any particular reason?'

'It's my name, eejit.'

'Rule Three,' says TJ, 'you don't speak to me or Mr McNulty 'less we address you first.'

'I wait for you guys to speak to me first.'

'And Rule Four,' goes Clinton, 'never go through a door before we go through first – got it?'

Laughing – louder than I meant! Their hackles rise, TJ leaning in close, sky and rock in his pale green eyes.

'Better wise up, boy. Me and Clinton are kings here, and we'll not have no sleazeball Dub shoving his weight around. Obey the rules and show proper respect and we'll rub along grand. Mess with us, and we'll mess with you, Jailchick, I promise.'

They hop down and swagger off. Everyone in class watching.

Shaking – shaking during project work and shaking all the way home with Peig. Still shaking lashing through homework. Normally I'd watch TV now, or play on my computer. But there's no TV and I'm shuffling into Peig's practice to e-mail Gerry –

* * *

Connemara calling!
Everything's cool. Aunt Peig not a witch –
real nice, and the place deadly – lame pig,
mad goat and a tame crow that sips tea! –
Sadie delighted with herself – only prob a
couple of little Hitlers at new school – trying
to boss me – wish you were here to help.

No, doesn't feel good talking about TJ and
Clinton. Somehow takes them too seriously,
gives them power. Delete that bit and send
the rest, plus 'PS – best to Miss Hart, Mr
Lucky and all in the gang – even Matty
Walsh.'

'Come on, Sadie! Going out for some air,
Auntie.'

'Want to take Brandy?'

'D'you think she'll come?'

Running, scattering hens, up the hill and
over the stone stile. 'Come on, Sadie, you can
do it! Show her, Brandy!'

Blanket cloud pressing down, spits of rain.
Splashing through fields.

'Look, Sadie! A donkey and her foal. Must be
Sunshine and Hiccups.' So beautiful with
their furry heads and placid eyes.

To reach Gabriel's sanctuary we cross a
stony track running with water, push through
a knot of trees and there, concealed by giant
rhubarb leaves and veiled in moss and ivy, is
the ancient well. Tacked to a tree, a picture of

117

Jesus and a little shelf crowded with sea-shells, bracelets, candle stubs. Tin cans, rusty and new, strung in low branches, knock and clink in the wind.

Clouds pressing down, rain coming harder. 'Come on, guys, let's go.'

Back home, try and distract myself with a fresh enactment of Waterloo, but through the smoke and stench and moans of the wounded I keep meeting the same cocky faces and sneers: Rule One, address TJ at all times as Boss; Two, Clinton as *Mr* McNulty; Three, never go through a door before them; Four, never speak to them unless they speak to you first – or was that Three?

Napoleon's gunners have just hit Sadie on the nose – 'Fools! *Imbéciles!* You couldn't heet a cow eef it shoved its 'ead in ze barrel of your cannon!'

No use. Heart's not in it. What do I do when they start on me tomorrow? Laugh in their faces?

Gorgeous blue morning, warm sun on the skin, views stretching for miles, kind of day when nothing bad can possibly happen. Ride the bus next to Hedgehog Thomas, who's going, 'Don't you play Gaelic in Dublin?' and 'When are you getting the full uniform?' and 'Are they going to beat you up, or what?'

'Did they make *you* call them Boss and Mr McNulty?'

'That's for new boys. We just get pushed around – it's nothing.'

Sticky Joe by the side of the road, getting on in his usual cagey way, grabbing the last empty seats. It's time I spoke to him.

'Telling you, Lorcan –' Thomas buzzing in my ear – 'you wanna do as they say if you like living.'

'Excuse us a sec,' says I, moving across to join Sticky Joe.

'Hi . . .'

'How's it goin'?' he mumbles, without looking.

119

'I'm Lorcan.'

'I worked that out.'

'You're Joe, right?'

'Joseph.'

Travelling in silence. Sun bouncing off school windows ahead. Through the glare, a gleaming Jag pulling up, TJ hopping out. The driver's Jack de Barra, who stood in court clapping Dad's sentence. Close behind, a hefty Land Cruiser flashing its lights, saying, *Hi!* to the Jag, Clinton in the passenger seat beside his big burly da, Willie-John McNulty, local TD.

'My advice, you wanna hit 'em quick and hard.'

'What's that?'

Joseph vaulting over me and off.

Strolling into school nice and easy, thinking about what he said: *My advice, hit 'em quick and hard.* No, it's all too ridiculous. I can't believe TJ and Clinton are really going to push that rules nonsense. It'll all calm down – or so I'm telling myself till I reach the classroom and find the way blocked.

'How's it going, Jailchick?' says TJ.

'Sorry?'

'I said, how's it going?'

Look them in the eye; think Che Guevara!

'Deadly!' trying to push past.

'Hold it!' Clinton sticking out his chest. 'We forgotten already?'

120

'Oh, sorry! It's *mister*, isn't it? Mr McNutty.'

'*McNulty!*'

'That's what I said, McNutty. And how was I supposed to address you, TJ? Buzz, wasn't it? Like, buzz off!' – pushing past.

Heart hammering, girls and boys looking at me in horror. Blue-eyed Courtney addressing Clinton: 'You going to let him away with that?'

Quick breaths carry me to my place. TJ sliding in beside me. 'Thought I told you: never go through a door first.'

'Thought I told you to buzz off.'

Veins throbbing in TJ's face. Like father, like son – mean and handsome.

Smiley whisper, 'We'll be waiting for you, Jailchick, after school.'

'Fine by me, Buzzy. But I'm not taking you two on together. We'll discuss it at break.'

'Discuss what, Jailchick?'

'Time, place and weapons.'

Must be stark raving mad. Never fought anyone in my life. Never had to. I'm not especially big or strong, but I must give off something that tells people to leave me alone, like a bright-coloured insect. Or used to.

And that girl Courtney – why's she siding with them? How many enemies have I got? Not Little Toad, pulling on her inhaler, looking round at me, worried her shiny knight's about to be knocked off his horse.

Miss Maddigan finishing the register, 'Now, who's giving a talk today?'

'Blaise,' groans Courtney.

'Oh no!' everyone echoing.

'That's quite enough, thank you!'

Blaise rising from her seat like a condemned prisoner, walking with dignity to the board; turns, clutching a roll of posters, pale as death. 'My talk is about—'

'Excuse me!'

'Sorry, miss. Good morning, class.'

'Good morning, Blaise,' everyone drones.

'I'm going to talk about Countess Markiewicz—'

'Must you?' Clinton from the back.

'Mr McNulty!'

'Well, miss, I'm bored already.'

'I'll have you know, young man, Constance Markiewicz is one of our greatest national heroes!'

'Did she play for Man United?'

Gales of laughter.

'No,' cries Blaise, 'she shot English soldiers dead!'

That shuts everyone up.

'She was a crack marksman. No better shot among the Irish rebels. And she certainly never would have played for an *English* football team, never mind supported one!'

Clinton blows a raspberry, Courtney rolls her eyes, but everyone else is hooked, and into the hush Blaise plunges –

'Countess Markiewicz was a high-born lady who was brought up in County Sligo. She joined the struggle to liberate Ireland from the British, who'd been brutally occupying us for hundreds of years. She wasn't afraid to get her hands bloody, or of what people would say about a lady wearing a major's uniform . . .'

She's fascinating – her accent, her passion, her big worried eyes. She's looking for helpers – Miss Maddigan beckons Little Toad and Hedgehog Thomas, who come out and stand like window dummies holding posters: Dublin on fire in 1916, Countess Markiewicz and sniper's rifle.

'Here's where she fought during the Rising –' Blaise stumbling on – 'holed up in the College of Surgeons in St Stephen's Green, HQ of the Citizens' Army, firing at the British in the Shelbourne Hotel – bullets whizzing over her head, and she never blinked, so she didn't—'

'Keep it brief,' Clinton groaning.

'Least she could shoot –' TJ teasing his pal – 'not like your useless Van Nistelrooy!'

'Quiet!' Miss Maddigan whacking the desk. 'Never interrupt a speaker!'

Blaise blinking, rushing on like a creature through fire – 'And after the surrender, she wept in jail listening to her comrades being executed, furious they wouldn't shoot her, just because she was a woman. After we won our Free State, she was elected to Westminster, first woman ever – but she refused to take her seat in the enemy's parliament, devoting the rest of her life to the poor and downtrodden, and on the day she died, she was carrying sacks of coal up to the poor of Dublin, and her funeral procession was the biggest Ireland had ever seen.'

'Is that it?' Clinton yawning.

'See me after, McNulty!' shrieks Miss Maddigan.

Blaise, breathless now, ending softly, fiercely, 'Countess Markiewicz is our Joan of Arc. It's a disgrace there isn't a statue of her in every town in Ireland; even bigger disgrace Hollywood hasn't bothered its arse to make a movie about her.'

'And no doubt you'd play her!' jeers TJ.

Hoots of laughter.

'I would too! Give me a few years!'

More laughter, and applause and cheers for Blaise. Even TJ's clapping, watching Blaise with unblinking eyes, and all at once I want to throttle him.

At break I follow her. Watch her disappear into the girls' toilets. Hang about the corridor pretending to be reading a notice. She reappears, looking green. I think she's been sick.

'Oh, hi! Just wanted to—'

She keeps walking. 'I need air.' First words we've spoken.

Outdoors, she flops against a wall with a book.

'What you reading?'

'*Julius Caesar*, a play by William Shakespeare.'

'Is it good?'

'Bits are good, bits are rubbish.'

'Don't hang round her, Jailchick –' TJ strolling over – 'she's mad and it's catching.'

'You and your stupid talk, McBride!' Clinton pointing. 'She's given me detention.'

'That all?' Blaise screwing up her nose. 'Should have drowned you at birth.'

Seething, 'One of these days, McBride . . .'

'Yeah, yeah, go change yer nappy.'

TJ laughing, 'Come on, Jailchick, serious business to discuss.' He and Clinton move away.

I'm looking at Blaise's bowed head. 'Just wanted to say your talk was great.'

'It was terrible.' She's lost in her book. I don't exist. Walking away to meet the enemy when she calls, 'What's your talk gonna be?'

'Che Guevara.'

'What? *Who?*'

'Never heard of Che Guevara?'

'Who was she?'

'*He!* You'll find out Friday.'

Drift over to where Courtney's joined TJ and Clinton on *my* wall, fixing me with a cool blue gaze.

'Just so you know whose pitch it is,' says TJ.

Easy laugh – shaking inside, 'You think because your bum's parked on a wall it's yours?'

'We own it,' says Clinton, ''cos we're kings of Raven Hill.'

'*Ha!*' I laugh, and at that, TJ hops down, pushes his nose into mine, same height and slender build, longish blond hair to my longish brown.

'You stink of Dublin, Jailchick, and we don't like yer snotty airs and snooty accent . . .'

'You tell him, TJ!' goes Courtney, obviously in love.

'You think you can muscle in on our show, you want your bum kicking.'

'Is that your proposal, Buzzy, a bum-kicking contest?'

Shoves me violently away. 'You think you're funny? We'll soon see who's laughing.'

Clinton jumping down, 'Come on, let's pick weapons!'

'What'll it be, Jailchick?'

'Whatever you like, Buzzy. How about chess?'

'*Chess?* Did he say chess?'

'He's taking the mick,' says Courtney.

'I'll box you,' says Clinton. 'Five rounds in Devil's Glen.'

126

'Fine by me.'

'You box?'

'All my life.'

Surprised. No wonder. I'm lying.

'Got your own gloves?'

'I will have.'

'That's you and Clint, Jailchick. What about you and me?'

'We'll draw lots.'

'Like how?'

'Ideas in a hat.'

Clinton runs to find pens and paper. Courtney sits on the wall kicking her legs. TJ and I hang loose, avoiding eyes. My outward coolness amazes me. TJ listening to my breathing.

'You really smoke Marlboros, Jailchick? You're crazy – they even kill grown-ups.'

'It's not ciggies,' says Courtney, 'that's asthma.'

Horror: 'Asthma?'

'Asthma, not leprosy,' says I. 'Che Guevara had it, and it didn't stop him.'

'Che G-*who*?'

Shocked! 'Never heard of Che Guevara?'

Clinton back in a sweat with pens and paper.

'Three ideas each,' TJ declares, tearing six strips of paper.

Turn our backs and start. How do I want to fight TJ? Toy soldiers and rubber bands?

'Time's up! Give us your first one, Jailchick.'

Still scribbling, 'Hang on a sec.'

'Come on!'

'OK – number one: arm wrestling.'

TJ shrugging, 'That'll do. Here's my first one – stones. Pile of stones each to throw at each other, till one of us is too hurt to carry on.'

'Fine,' says I, remembering my skills hurling cricket balls and skimming stones at the beach.

'Next, Jailchick.'

'Taking penalties.'

'Forget it, that's football, not fighting. My number two – bare-knuckle fighting.'

'No bare fists, I play piano.'

'Ooh, he plays piano!' jeers Courtney.

'Nah, he's right,' says TJ. 'I play cello. Musician's got to mind his hands. What's your last one, Jailchick?'

'Duel scene from *El Cid*.'

'*What!*'

'It's a film with jousting on horseback I used to watch with my dad.'

'Before he went to jail!' laughs Clinton.

'Horses?' TJ frowning. 'Who the hell's going to lend us horses?'

'We'll improvise!'

Courtney: 'Impro-*what*?'

'Make do with whatever's handy.'

128

'Like what, Jailchick?'

'Ride on someone's shoulders, with branches for lances.'

'Mmm, that'd be a good crack.'

'I'll be your horse, TJ!' says Clinton.

'Yeh, you'd make a good horse. OK, my last one – dinghy wrestling. Sail into the estuary and try and knock each other into the water. Can you swim? Good! Let's pick!' Screwing up the scraps of paper, 'Go on, Clinty.'

'No,' I object; 'someone neutral.'

'*Someone neutral . . . no bare fists!*' goes Courtney. 'What a geek!'

Looking around for someone suitable, 'Blaise!'

'Don't trust her,' says TJ. 'Sticky Joe. He won't blab.'

Buzzer's going: end of break.

Hurrying over to where Joseph's bouncing a baldy tennis ball. TJ holding out his fist, 'Pick one, Sticky.'

'What for?'

'See which way I'm going to thrash this mouthy Dub.'

Joseph looking at me, like, *Do you know what you're getting into?*

Shrug and smile – no worries. TJ opening his fist, Joseph stirring the balls of paper, grabs one, opens it, squints: '*Penalties.*'

'Nah, we got rid of that one,' says TJ. 'Pick again.'

Joseph picks another – *'Bare-knuckle fighting.'*

'Got rid of that too. Again!'

Picks a third. *'Duel scene from* El Cid.'

'Will you boys get into class!' Miss Maddigan!

'El Cid it is!' says TJ.

'Just name the day, Jailchick,' says Clinton.

'I'm not fighting you both the same day.'

'El Cid after school tomorrow,' says TJ.

'Make it Friday. I've got a talk to prepare.'

'Box you Monday,' says Clinton, rubbing his hands in glee.

'I'll ref,' says Joseph; 'make sure there's no dirty business.'

The long day drags on in a blur of terror, TJ and Clinton strutting like kings of the dung hill, following me with mocking eyes. Gaze back cool as a breeze, trying to plant doubt in their minds. Secretly – in the jacks, round deserted corners – take deep pulls on the inhaler, desperate to get through the day.

What have I done? Two days to prepare a talk on a dead hero I hardly know anything about, and straight into battle with TJ, who's talking about welding swords at home out of lengths of steel building rod. Survive that one, and I'm boxing Clinton in Devil's Glen – wherever that is – when I've never thrown a punch in my life.

Be realistic – pursue the impossible!
Taking pulls on the inhaler as Peig drives me home.

'You all right, honey?'

'Fine thanks, Auntie.'

'Go easy on that thing,' rooting out a mobile and dialling.

Gasping, 'Shouldn't drive and make calls, Auntie.'

Pulling over, brakes screeching, 'Quite right, hon, only I promised your ma I'd call nice Dr— Betty? Peig Lynch. Could Dr Sweeney take a look at my nephew when he has a minute?'

Flying along with rocky fields and sparkling water left and right, lungs grating, brain spinning with visions of Clinton and TJ coming at me from all angles.

Breathless – 'My talk's on Friday, Auntie – Che Guevara.'

'Good for you! I might even lend you my beret!'

Good to be home, high hedge and honeysuckle, meadowy lawn and unlocked door. Peig helping me onto the couch, mopping my hot brow, her assistant Sadie licking the sweat off my face. By the time the doorbell rings, I'm calm, breathing easier, determined to enjoy my last few days on this planet.

'Ted Lynch's lad – delighted!' says Doc Sweeney. He's tall and stout with silvery hair, and the way he looks at my aunt, I've a feeling he's glad of this excuse to call on her.

'I've a daughter Katie your age, Lorcan. Lives with her mother in America. Mad into horse riding and conservation – can't keep up with her.'

Humming a merry tune as he examines me.

'Isn't my nephew a grand lad, Brendan?'

'Bit thin. Aren't you feeding him, woman?'

'Healthy thin. Preferable to *over*eating, don't you think?'

'Ooh, did you hear that, Lorcan? The cruelty of women! Hmm –' tapping my chest – 'lungs under stress, but the pulse is sure and the heart strong.'

'He's giving a talk at school on Che Guevara.'

'Good man yourself. My great-aunt Rosie dashed over to play fiddle in this very room that night.'

'He was a doctor too, wasn't he, Doctor?' proud of my new knowledge. 'And asthmatic.'

'Indeed he was, and maintained that in the Sierra Maestra his inhaler was as handy as his rifle!'

'Don't encourage him, Brendan, I'm trying to wean him off.'

'Don't tell me you're thinking of sticking your dreaded needles in this poor boy? Don't let her, Lorcan! She'll make a pincushion out of you.'

132

'He wouldn't be the first asthmatic I've treated.'

'Your sweet but misguided aunt suffers from an exaggerated faith in Chinese medicine.'

Peig laughing, 'And this charming but confused doctor seriously believes his drugs cure.'

'I may have my faults, Peig, but being wrong isn't one of them.'

I lie on the couch listening to radio while Peig and Doc Sweeney dine in the kitchen, teasing each other.

Drag myself into Peig's practice to gen up on my old pal Che.

Terror making me light-headed and dizzy, sitting on the grass verge feeling naked and exposed.

Riding the school bus in a trance, hoping that after I've been mangled by TJ and murdered by Clinton, my new classmates will at least respect me for trying.

There's Joseph, standing by the road like a sentinel. Picks a window seat alone. Looks round, making signs: *Come here.*

Me? Get up and join him.

'Ever boxed before?'

'No.'

Frown of utter disbelief. 'And you're gonna box McNulty?'

'Yes.'

'You're going climb into a ring with a boy who's been swinging punches since he was six?'

'Quick and hard, that's what you told me.'

'Yeah, but sly and dirty – jump out and poke

134

'em in the eye, or whack 'em round the head with a hurling stick.'

Riding in silence.

'You box, Joseph?'

'Same club as him. Snooty scumbags.'

'Who?'

'Tried to stop me joining. Didn't want a filthy traveller in their club. Me da threatened to take 'em to court, and they bellied out, and I went in and skinned every one of their poxy boxers. All except McNulty. We bloodied each other up pretty good.'

'Could you teach me?'

Looking at me for the first time, his eyes and face very still, carved out of Connemara stone with red eyebrows. One hand, I notice, is relaxed. The other's a fist.

'When's the fight?'

'Monday.'

Laughs, 'Monday? And today's Thursday?'

Feel sick. See myself jumping the coach to Galway, the train to Dublin, Maria moving in to mind me. Sorry, Ma, couldn't hack it.

'Meet you after school.'

'What? My auntie picks me up.'

'Give her a ring.'

'I don't bring a mobile to school.'

Slipping me a bulky out-of-date mobile, 'Tell her you'll be late. Meet ye on the bus. Keep it hush.'

* * *

135

No escape from my tormentors – TJ leaning in whispering, 'Give yourself a break, Jailchick. Call me Boss, and we'll live happily ever after.'

OK, boss, anything you say – why won't it come out?

'Thanks for the offer, Buzzie, but you'll have to kill me first.'

Clinton brushing past me in the jacks, 'No need to get stuffed, Jailchick. Call me Mister and everything's hunky dory!' Off he goes laughing, a few others too, 'cos it's safer to laugh with the predator than run with the prey.

Phone Peig on Joseph's mobile. Some lame excuse about football training.

'OK, hon. Call me, I'll pick you up.'

School day's over at last. Waiting in the crowd for the bus, Joseph pretending he doesn't know me. He's forgotten, embarrassed, changed his mind.

On the bus he slides in beside me.

'Here,' says I, trying to return the mobile.

'Not now.'

Pulling up somewhere called Nook. 'Hop off quick,' he whispers; 'take the Cashelbreen road.'

Confused, I get off with a few others, see sign for Cashelbreen and start walking. And walking – hot sun on my neck, terror in my

136

throat. Alone on an empty road surrounded by bleached boulders and wild hedges bursting with blood-red fuchsias and suddenly, on the rise – a rider. Closer and it's Joseph astride a black and white pony, a rug for saddle, two pairs of red boxing gloves strung round his neck.

'Hop up on the wall and get on behind me.'

Climb onto the low, jagged wall. Joseph manoeuvres the pony alongside, but it keeps shifting. 'I don't think I can do it.'

'And ye wanna fight that thug McNulty? Jump!'

Leap, land with a bump and cling to Joseph.

Clicks his tongue, wheels the pony round and away up the road we trot – *up-down, up-down*, the animal's hard back thumping my bum.

'Why don't you want to be seen with me? You ashamed of me?'

'You want them to know I'm training you?'

'Yes!'

Swinging the pony off the road into a sea of gorse and fern, narrow zigzagging tracks all leading to a cottage sheltering under an old tree crawling with ravens. Closer and the dwelling is a ruin with no roof – relic from the famine? – the tree growing inside, spreading through the empty shell. Ravens lift off like black flapping handkerchiefs, lazily beating the air over the fields. Through gaping windows, the estuary running out to sea.

'This is it.'

'This is what?'

'Our own private gym.'

Jump down. Pony starts grazing, big placid eyes.

'What's his name?'

'It's *her* name, and it's Ginny Jo.'

Ginny Jo, kidspeak for dandelion.

Flings a pair of gloves at me. Struggle into them, and he ties them for me, lacing his own with his teeth, hair red as dried blood, eyes grey-green as the estuary, face moulded into high cheeks and a flat nose.

'Why don't we use your club?'

'Clinton trains there. Better he don't see us.'

'Why?'

'Your only hope is surprise.' *Bang!* Hits me in the face.

'Ow! What was—?'

Bang! Again – and again, knocking me sideways. Head reeling.

'Come on, defend yerself! That's it – block me! Hit me!'

No use, his punches are too quick and sharp. Another hit and I'm stumbling backwards through the missing door of the ruin, flat on my back.

'You didn't give me a chance!'

'You think Clinton's gonna give you a chance?'

Helping me up. Head throbbing, face stinging. Feel like whacking him with a broken branch.

'Hit me,' he says, dropping his arms. 'Hard as you can.'

Swing . . . and miss. Swing again; he leans away.

'Come on, ye wuzzie! Hit me – or get back to Dublin!'

Right! That's it – fired up and crashing after him, swinging wildly, until at last one punch smashes into his face, and he winces, falls.

He's really mad, going to jump up and hammer me. No he's not – he's smiling as he gets up. 'So you *can* punch. Hit my glove!' he says, holding one up.

Swing! He whips the glove away. Keep swinging and he keeps moving, and now I'm chasing him in and out the ruins, throwing punches and running out of breath – fumbling for the inhaler.

'Stop!' checking his watch. 'You lasted three minutes. Clinton's planning five rounds, three minutes each. That's fifteen minutes.'

'I'll never last, will I?'

'No.'

Slump against wall. It's hopeless. Feel the rough, mossy stone warm on my hands, walls inhabited long ago by people who woke up one morning with nothing to eat. A wasp – drawn to my sweat – fans my forehead.

'Come on, get up, work to do.'

'What's the point, if I'm going to lose?'

'Who said?'

'You admitted I won't last five rounds.'

'That's why you got to beat him in two. Or one. No –' thinking it through – 'two.'

Spar for another hour. Lungs hurt, but they're loving it, pumping air.

'Forget the boxing for a minute,' says Joseph, halo of midges round his head. 'You need a horse for tomorrow's fight with TJ. Hop up!'

Round and round the ruins we go, me on his back and he whooping and shouting; catches his foot, down we crash in a heap – *ow-wow-wouch!* – laughing our sides sore.

Joseph in the ruins picking juicy leaves for Ginny Jo, me trawling for dead wood, selecting a straight enough branch, and away we go again, charging up and down, Joseph getting used to my weight, me grasping him with one hand, the lance with the other, aiming at a pair of boxing gloves in a bush – *dun-dee-dun-dee-dun* – *Stab!* 'Die, TJ, die!'

Whoops! Look at the time.

Sun starting to dip when finally we trot up the lane to Skylarks. Peig in the doorway, arms folded. 'It's after seven. Where you been?'

Car bouncing up the track, out jumps Doc Sweeney: 'Been looking for you everywhere.'

140

'I was about to call the guards,' says Peig. First time I've seen her cross, except for a second that first night when she talked about the planned new road.

Slide down from pony. Joseph whirls round and gallops off in a cloud of stones.

'I'm sorry, Auntie. Dr Sweeney. Down, Sadie, down! Joseph and I were practising for, um, a big match on Monday.'

'Look at your uniform!'

Eat my dinner, soak aching limbs in bath, collapse into bed.

'You had me worried' – Peig, tucking me in.

'I'm sorry.'

'Next time you and your friend want to practise, do it here, OK?' Kisses my brow, ruffles Sadie's head and goes to leave.

'Auntie.'

'Yes?'

'I'm in trouble.'

'At school?' Sitting on my bed, 'What is it?'

Want to tell her how TJ's going to scar me for life, and Clinton's going to put me in hospital, but one disaster at a time – 'My Che Guevara talk's first thing after register, and I've only got a few boring facts.'

'We'll have breakfast early. I might have a few surprises.'

12

Waiting by the road, sleepy-eyed – Peig had me up at six! Queasy belly, thumping heart. This must be how condemned men feel on their last morning.

Sun peeling away the mist, the bus ghosting out of a mirage.

Heart beating so hard, the windows of the bus are rattling. Let me off! I want to lie in a cool ditch and dream. Nerves jangling, listening to Che Guevara on a Walkman, a few minutes of his voice captured on Grandad's tape recorder, transferred years later to cassette.

Joseph getting on, sits alone, ignoring me. Glances round, quick eye contact, telling me everything's cool. Doesn't want word to reach Clinton's ears that Jailchick Lynch is ready.

Me, ready?

Getting off, there's TJ calling us over. Clinton lifting a roll of canvas out of his da's Land Cruiser.

'All set for after school, Jailchick?' opening the roll to reveal two motorbike helmets, two dustbin lids, four branches for lances, and swords made out of thin building rods, handles secured with wire. 'Had the gardener make them – cool, huh?'

'Come on, move it, lads,' big, bullish Willie-John McNulty running round to slam the boot. 'Enjoy the play or whatever! Be a good boy, son,' clipping Clinton round the head. Away in a cloud of fumes.

'Come on, Clint, we got to hide this.'

'Want a hand?' says I.

'No.'

Watch them running off round the side of the school, carrying the weapons between them.

Miss Maddigan stifling a weary end-of-week yawn, beckoning me with curling finger, 'Is your talk ready, Lorcan?'

Whispering in her ear.

'Hmm, interesting; off you go then.'

Make my way to the toilets, lungs starting to break down. Changing into shirt and jeans that were pale blue till Peig tie-dyed them into army fatigues. Fasten bandolier across chest – Peig up half the night sewing it, complete with paper bullets painted gold. Squeezing into her leather boots. Spread glue on face, attach flimsy beard and moustache made of lamb's wool dyed black. Finally the famous beret, with red star attached. Stand back – *Wow!* It's him, aged sixteen! Handsome, fierce, invincible. My followers will love me – my enemies will quake in their boots.

Frantic pulls on my inhaler as I return down empty corridors.

Rap-rap! on door – enter puffing pretend cigar.

Room falls still. Eyes popping.

'Señor Guevara!' cries Miss Maddigan. 'What an unexpected honour.'

'*Buenos días, Señora Maddigan, buenos días*, class. My talk today is about myself –' borrowing Maria's Latin American accent – 'how I was born in Argentina, a sickly asthmatic boy on the fourteenth of May, nineteen twenty-eight; how my father's name was Don Ernesto Guevara *Lynch*; how I grew up to love freedom and hate injustice; how I liberated Cuba from nasty dictator Fulgencio Batista; how I visited Ireland in nineteen sixty-five and spent the night in the humble home of Patrick Lynch – grandfather of Lorcan Lynch – and died two years later trying to bring revolution to poverty-stricken Bolivia—'

'What you doing talking to us if you're dead?' says TJ.

'Questions at the end!' snaps Miss Maddigan.

'I'm a spirit!' I reply.

'It's a ghost – *wooo!*' – Clinton from the back.

'*Wooo-wooo!*' Others taking up the chant.

Miss Maddigan's trying to quell them, but it's such fun and now the panic's rising, demons loose in my chest, squeezing the air out of me.

'We sailed for Cuba in a leaky old boat called the Grandma. Storms blew us off course, straight into the arms of the army—'

'Naughty-naughty!'

'We lost most of our men and I was wounded—'

'In the head!'

'And fled into the Sierra Maestra, where we became guerrillas marching all night and striking at dawn—'

Chest-beating and monkey hoots.

'Will you be quiet!' cries Miss Maddigan.

'*Oohoo-oohoo!*' Courtney leading the apes.

'Shuddup!' someone yells – Blaise! 'This is good!' Applause for Blaise!

'Thank you, Miss McBride, I think I can handle my own class.'

Stumble on, room spinning, lungs cracking up.

'Have *you* got asthma too?' asks Little Toad.

'Questions at the *end*, Róisín!'

'Sorry, miss.'

Getting serious, someone trying to shove my head under water. Turn away, deep pull on inhaler.

'*Ha!* Did Che Guevara carry one of them?'
TJ laughs.

'Yes! Inhaler in one hand, gun in the other –' rambling blindly now, no Latin accent, no focus – 'and he and Fidel Castro thrashed Batista, and set up a new government – clinics, schools—'

'*Booo!*'

'And Che travelled the world preaching revolution – got stranded in Ireland, bumped into my dad and Aunt Peig by the side of the road—'

'Did he run them over?'

'Grandad invited him in for dinner and a sing-song and he slept in the bed I sleep in now . . .'

Clinton pretending to puke, 'Yuck! Sharing a bed with a gorilla!'

I've got Blaise holding up the photo of Che and my family, and the tape running, a few crackly moments of his actual voice – soft and deep, discussing pipes and cigars with my grandad: half the class riveted, others laughing at Dad in short trousers who'll end up one day in the slammer . . . I'm going under, holding onto a desk, noticing Little Toad having trouble breathing, Joseph puzzled, Blaise pale . . . last thing I'm thinking as the floor comes up to hit me: *Will she ever fancy me after this?*

Panic in the classroom – bodies leaping, underwater voices.

Clumsy arms lifting me out – *bang!* into a door – not the smooth teamwork of old, fighting for air, nothing but dust. I'm burning up and drowning, a sailor in blazing oil . . .

Cool, delicious oxygen, and this time it's Miss Maddigan and Doc Sweeney leaning over me, removing the mask—

'Breathing's regular, temperature nearly normal. You could go straight into battle, Señor Guevara!'

'I intend to, Doctor.'

He thinks I'm joking.

Back in class, expecting scorn, everyone's friendly.

'Brill talk, Lorcan!'

'Deadly outfit!'

'That asthma attack –' Little Toad excited – 'I thought you were acting. You went a fierce weird colour.'

Joseph's hand on my arm. 'You up to fighting later?'

'I think so.'

'Think so?'

'I'm sure.'

'Good, 'cos you're gonna waste him!'

His confidence thrills – and scares – me.

Another hand on my arm – Blaise, whispering, 'Spoke to me da. He knew all about Che Guevara! But we got to talk – it's real important.'

147

'Welcome back, Lorcan!' Enter Miss Maddigan, all dramatic, placing one hand on my shoulder, the other on her heart. 'I am teaching a boy touched by history!'

'Does that mean it's not such a bad thing having asthma, miss?' says Little Toad.

'Afflictions can be gifts, Róisín, if they make you stronger and wiser. Now, it's time for Irish.'

'Ahh, miss, can't we hear more about Shaker Mara?'

'It's Che Guevara, Thomas, and take out your Irish.'

Groans all round. Miss Maddigan's high, clear voice: *Ní h-é lá na gaoithe lá na scolb!*

Blaise making signs at me, *Talk to you after*.

'Miss McBride! Translate, if you please.'

'Um – *The boys and girls in Miss Maddigan's class are angels.*'

'Nice try, but we weren't listening, were we? Lorcan, you try.'

'*Seamos realistas – pidamos lo imposible!*'

'I beg your pardon?'

'It's Spanish, miss. Means, *Be realistic – pursue the impossible!*'

Laughs! 'Where on earth did you get that from? Róisín.'

'*The windy day is not the thatching day!*'

'Thank you! In other words, girls and boys, don't leave it to the last minute to revise for your exams.'

Rush of bodies round the back after school –
'Quick! Before anyone sees us!' Somehow the
word's out – even kids from other classes have
heard: TJ de Barra's fighting the new boy!
Told Peig I was playing a match. Maybe
everyone's using the same fib.

Eager mob pouring across the back road
and down the steep slope into Devil's Glen,
TJ's noisy followers leading the stampede,
then me – head and lungs cleared by the
attack – escorted by Joseph and Blaise, Róisín
panting behind.

I really don't want to lose, not in front of
everyone, especially Blaise.

'Got to talk to you after, Lorcan.'

'Can we get through this first?'

'It's real important.'

'OK, if I'm still alive.'

Down we slide into a valley trapped
between rocky slopes. At the bottom a ring
of wrecked cars, beaten up and rusted. It's

here the weapons are hidden.

It's all happening too fast: TJ's on Clinton's back, jockeying up and down in shiny white helmet and visor, Courtney – his number one admirer – handing him his lance. 'Where do the swords go, Jailchick?'

Swords look clumsy and vicious – can't believe we're going to use them. 'Um, not sure.'

'Not sure?' shouts Clinton. 'It was your idea, eejit!'

Don't like being shown up in front of people. Blood starting to boil.

'Do it yourself, Clinton, if you're so clever!' cries Blaise.

'Ah, shuddup, stupid cow!'

'Cow's fine by me –' Blaise running at Clinton, flinging out a foot, sending horse and rider tumbling to the ground – 'but *stupid* you can keep!'

Shrieks of laughter round the gorge, Little Toad going, 'Shhhh, we'll get caught,' and Courtney going mad, catching Blaise round the neck, choking her. Want to run and rescue her, but a kick from Blaise has Courtney hopping around going, 'Owww, you cow, I'll kill ye!'

Everyone creased up laughing.

'*Shhhhh!*' pleads Little Toad.

TJ remounting, 'The swords, Jailchick!'

'Right!' says I, plunging the swords into

boggy ground twenty paces apart, calling, 'If
both riders are still in the saddle after the
first charge, then ride on, round the sword
and charge again.'

TJ donning his shiny helmet, resting his
lance on Clinton's shoulder. My helmet's
scarred, with a scratched blurry visor. Couple
of pulls on my inhaler and climb on Joseph's
back. He grips me under the bum and gets
comfy. Blaise handing me a brittle-looking
branch and battered bin lid. 'How come TJ
gets all the flash equipment?' she objects.

' 'Cos I'm king,' declares TJ, 'and Jailchick's
a dirty Dub!'

'Start us off, Blaise,' shouts Joseph.

'OK. Ready, TJ?'

'Let battle commence!'

'Ready, Lorcan?'

Looking into Blaise's eyes: 'Knights go into
battle with a lady's colours on their lance, a
bright scarf or something.'

Cheers and whistles.

'Nobody's wearing scarves, eejit!' says
Courtney.

'Something else then.'

'Knickers!' someone shouts. Everyone
falling about.

'Get on with it!' Clinton shouting. 'He's getting heavy.'

Blaise offering her sock.

'Sock'll do fine,' says I.

151

To groans of horror, Blaise whips off a grubby mauve sock with holes in, ties it to the tip of my lance, hissing, 'You can do it, Che!'

Blood rushing to my head.

'What about me?' TJ huffs. 'Which fair lady will lend hers?'

'Get stuffed!' girls shriek, but Courtney's dragging off a clean white sock, tying it to TJ's lance.

Blaise's hand held high. 'Get set – go!'

Whoah! Joseph leaps forwards, throwing me backwards – crashing to the ground. Crowd explodes with laughter. Sitting up dazed, lance and shield in hand. Clinton sinking to his knees, laughing, TJ rolling over in fits.

Blaise and Róisín helping me back onto Joseph. Blaise calling us to order again: 'Ready – go!'

I throw my weight forward this time, galloping over the ground with TJ galloping towards me, lance aimed at his body, his at mine, stumbling nearer and nearer. *Crash!* into his shield, he into mine – only my lance snaps!

'Keep going, Joseph!' – to the opposite sword, where Blaise flings me a spare lance, and back into a gallop we go to roars of encouragement, Clinton bearing down on us, TJ's lance coming at my face. I meet it with my shield and catch him in the ribs – a howl and he's down, cursing and holding his side.

Crowd holds its breath. Joseph throws me off and raises a fist. 'Lorcan wins!'

Clinton pointing, 'Shuddup, knacker!'

The word hangs in the air. Joseph throws a fist, Clinton goes down – bounces up with bloody lip, bundles Joseph over and pummels him with punches – Joseph rolling this way and that to save himself – Blaise dragging Clinton off, Courtney flinging herself at Blaise and me hollering, 'Swords! We haven't finished!'

'Which one do we go for?' cries TJ, holding his side.

'Whichever's nearest – you OK?'

Both of us dash for the same one, arriving at the same time – TJ barging me out the way, tearing the sword from the ground and chasing me like a dervish.

'*Ow!*' – stabbed in the leg.

'Touché!' he cries. 'Hands up! Surrender!'

'*Yield!* you're meant to shout,' says I.

'OK, *yield* then!'

'No!' seizing his sword hand, grapple visor to visor, staggering round together till –

'*Damn!*' He slips, and I sprint for the other sword, drag it out of the ground and lift it just in time to take a heavy blow. *Ping!* A volley of blows on sword and shield – *Ping! Clunk! Ping!* TJ on fire, driving me backwards into the ring of wrecked cars, the crowd roaring us on: 'Go on, TJ!' 'Hit him, Lorcan!'

153

'Wait!' I bawl.

'What?' he cries and stops, sword raised, while I take a pull on my inhaler.

'OK!'

Round the rusty ring we go, TJ raining blows, me fending them off, scrambling backwards to escape, up onto the crushed wing and dented roof of a Volkswagen shell, and down the other side, with TJ roaring and laughing, 'Yield, ye dirty Dub!' – cockier by the second, flinging away his shield and starting to lift off his helmet, the better to see me, when his foot drops into a gaping windscreen . . . drops his sword to break his fall. He's at my mercy.

Stand over him, sword poised, Blaise's sock in his face, 'Yield!'

'Never!'

'I say yield!'

'And I say never!'

'Someone's coming!' Róisín wails.

'Ah, shuddup, Fatso!' says Courtney, but Róisín's right: Mr Trench is on the skyline shielding his eyes –

'What on earth is going on down there?'

A football magically appears.

'Just a practice match, sir!' TJ calls.

'You've got one minute to get out!'

Gone. *Phew!* Phone's ringing, Blaise digging out a mobile. 'It's me da. Anyone want a lift?'

* * *

TJ's mum waiting in a shiny red BMW, trendy blonde hair and shades. TJ laughing and joking, pointing at me. 'You were dead lucky, Lynchy!'

'So it's Lynchy now – what happened to Jailchick?'

'You'll need more than luck on Monday, *Jailchick!*' Clinton waving an unfriendly fist.

'Come on, boys, for goodness' sake, where have you been?' Mrs de Barra banging the wheel.

'I told you we'd be late, Ma!'

'Not this late, I'm here twenty minutes.'

TJ and Clinton climb in the back and the BMW takes off like a jet from an aircraft carrier.

Blaise's dad leans on a muddy old Saab folding a newspaper: rugged-looking fellow wearing denim and sandals and specs on his nose; hippy hard-man with wind-burned smile.

'Hi, Da. You waiting long?'

'I dunno!' swapping kisses. 'Couple of hours.'

'Oh yeah! Couple o' minutes, more like.' She loves him – I'm jealous.

'Hop in, everyone. Excuse the squash. I'm Finbar. Who are all you?'

'Da, this is Joseph – he's a traveller; and Róisín – she's, um, deadly at Irish . . .' Joseph blinks, Róisín blushes. 'And this is Lorcan.'

155

'Ah, Lorcan, I'm a big fan of your dad. How's he coping, if you don't mind me asking?'

'I think he's doing OK; hard to tell.'

'That performance in court! Priceless.'

Whistling tunelessly as he turns the engine and pumps pedals, the Saab winding itself up like someone trying to sneeze. 'Come on, girl, these lads want to get home. Was it a good match, or whatever?'

'Told you, Da, it was combat, like knights of old, Lorcan on Joseph's back, TJ on Clinton's, followed by a vicious sword fight. It was *deadly*! Wish it could have been me they insulted.'

'You mean a proper organized brawl? Who won, dare I—?'

'Lorcan, of course, and Joseph, his trusty steed.'

Finbar beating the wheel in delight. 'De Barra and McNulty's boys hammered – great stuff!'

'She's going to kill me,' bleats Róisín as we pull up outside a tidy bungalow with B&B sign in the garden.

Peering from window, not looking pleased – Mrs Toad!

'Thanks for the lift.'

On we go, me in the back with Joseph, Blaise twisting round. 'I got to talk to you, Lorcan. Give us your number.'

Pulling up at Skylarks, Blaise's da says, 'Are they bullying you, Lorcan?'

156

'No – well, a bit.'

'You want me to talk to the school?'

'Thanks, but I can handle it.'

'You keep an eye, Blaise, you hear?'

'I am doing, Da.'

Joseph kicking his heels. Me waving as the Saab U-turns away down the track. Pushing open the gate, whispering, 'Look, Joseph! Freddie the fearless pheasant.'

Joseph laughs uneasily. 'See them all the time.' Freddie skips away round a hedge.

Inside, glimpse Peig at work in her doctor's white coat, sticking needles in wild man Gabriel's bony chest. 'Hi, Auntie!'

'Hiya, hon. How did Che go down?'

'Brilliant – thanks to you. I got Joseph with me.'

'Hi, Joseph. Make yourselves at home.'

Take cold drinks out back, introduce Joseph to the mad menagerie of residents, but he seems uncomfortable, ignoring Sadie bounding up to greet us, and Prudence sniffing his heels. 'I forgot the gloves.'

'What? That mean we can't train?'

Thinks . . . 'Nah, who needs gloves!'

Working in the barn, me throwing combination punches at his open hands, sharpening reflexes, burning my knuckles and bruising his palms.

Doubled up, fighting for breath. 'Be honest, Joseph. I'm never going to beat him, am I?'

157

'Told you, I got a plan.'

'What is the plan?'

'You'll see.' Jumping up, 'I got to go.'

'Stay for dinner.'

'No. But thanks.' Won't even take a lift. Throws a wave and sets out walking the three or four miles home.

Wheezing from dust and hay and animal hairs as I watch him go. I've a feeling this was his first visit to a classmate's home.

Phone goes early next morning.

'Young lady for you, hon – and I don't mean your ma!'

Blaise! 'We got to meet! Can I come over?'

Finbar drops her off. Blaise McBride, freckles and easy smile, stepping into the house. Hair fresh-washed and pretty earrings. 'Hello, Mrs Lynch!'

Peig clasping Blaise's hands, 'I've heard so much about you.'

'Yeah? I've only known Lorcan a week.'

'Well, you've made quite an impression.'

Looking around, 'This where you had the sing-song with Che Guevara?'

'He danced with my mother right where you're standing. Let me squeeze you kids some juice.'

Blaise is wearing jeans, plain white gym shoes and a T-shirt saying REVENGE! showing a terrified huntsman chased by a pack of foxes. Staring at my Nike trainers, dark

159

eyebrows swooping, 'You wear that trash?'

'Um . . .'

'Doesn't it bother you wearing stuff made by slave labour in faraway countries?'

'Well . . .'

'And making yourself look like every other sheep-brained eejit?'

'You sound like my dad.'

'Come and get it!' Peig to my rescue. 'Looks like blood, but it's only carrot and beetroot.'

Peig's going shopping, the place is ours. I show Blaise out the back.

'Jeez! Look at this!' Blaise amazed, delighted.

Introduce her to Noel the crow, strutting about like a park warden, Prudence limping over for a scratch, Ginger curled up like a glove in the woodpile, and Sally the goat rubbing her back on a post – and here's Sadie loping over to greet us.

'Wow! What a dog! He yours?'

'She. Sadie, meet Blaise.'

'You're only gorgeous!' she says, getting her arms scratched and her face licked.

Sitting together on a log surrounded by twittering, grunting creatures, Sadie's head in Blaise's lap. 'Boy, people take to you fast, Blaise.'

'Hate me fast too,' stroking Sadie's head.

'What did you want to see me about?' I ask.

'You like animals, Lorcan?'

'Sure, why?'

'You know TJ's da has an island?'

'I think I've seen it, from up there.'

'Show us!'

Running up the slope, over the stone stile, me and my lungs trying to match Blaise to the top of the hill. The sea wide and endless, the sky glorious blue, except where gigantic clouds are rolling in, like a mountain range on the move, sunny on top, black beneath and sheeting down to touch the sea, like downwards paint strokes applied by an invisible hand. 'Amazing sky, Blaise.'

'Rain, coming this way.'

'How can you tell?'

'Those dark lines falling.'

Never seen that before, curtain of rain coming from miles away, rushing towards us.

Blaise pointing, 'Inishbán – that's it. Looks nice and peaceful, doesn't it?'

'Isn't it?'

'Are you crazy? It's a prison camp!'

'Prison camp?'

'I don't suppose Jack de Barra's party guests notice a thing, as they sip cocktails on the terrace, but out across the island, animals are being starved and beaten. Inishbán's a concentration camp!' she says, talking fast and furious. 'They're helpless over there, Lorcan – kicked and starved and left out in freezing rain, and when he slaughters them,

161

he doesn't do it properly, he gets drunk and chases hens, ducks – I've even seen him chase a sheep and smash it over the head—'

'Hey, slow down . . . are we talking about Jack de Barra?'

'No, his caretaker, Jethro Dobbs – Deathrow Dobbs, I call him. Gets crazy drunk and runs round kicking the animals, roaring at them and laughing. You can hear his laugh on the wind sometimes, and the gun he uses to kill the sheep, or any bird unlucky enough to fly over.'

'Hang on, Blaise – how do you know all this?'

'You think I'm making it up? Is that what you think?'

'No, but it sounds . . .'

'Sounds what? Like loopy Blaise and her crazy animal stuff?'

'I'm not saying that, I'm just asking—'

'I live opposite the island, right, and I've been watching through my da's binoculars and keeping a diary since January last year – sixteen months, three weeks and five days, if you want to know.'

'What kind of animals we talking about, apart from sheep?'

'Ponies and donkeys that once belonged to TJ, his sister and cousins. There used to be loads of them – now there's just one pony and two donkeys – and they didn't all die of old age, I'm telling you, and from what I can see on clear days across the water, the remaining ones look pitiful. He keeps dogs, and they all move real slow, and he's got ducks and hens he only feeds when he's fattening them for the pot.'

'Sounds horrible.'

'I go to bed at night thinking about those animals just across the water and I can't sleep.'

'Does TJ know about all this? Does his dad know?'

'I've said to TJ many times, *Do you realize Dobbs beats and kicks those animals?* and he says, like you said, *How d'you know?* And I tell him like I told you, *I've seen it over and over through binoculars*, and you know what he says? He says, *You shouldn't be spying!* And I say, *That's not spying, that's doing the right thing!* And he says, *You shouldn't be meddling in other people's affairs.* And I say, *Cruelty to animals is everybody's affair*, and he says, *Mind your own business.* And I say, *I'm making it my business*, and he just laughs and says, *Get lost!* But I won't get lost, Lorcan – no way.'

'But does TJ's dad know?'

'I'm sure he does, but he's away mostly.'

'Have you informed the authorities?'

'Loads of times, but somehow Dobbs gets word they're coming, does just enough to

163

make the animals look cared for, and gets away with a warning.'

'Do people know about it?'

'Everyone knows, but who cares about a few mistreated animals? Jack de Barra's God round here – great man for gifts and favours.'
First drops of rain shining on Blaise's cheeks.

'Have you been over and seen any cruelty?'

'How can I? The island's private, and the ferry, which only goes once a week, is private too. But that's my aim: get over and take pictures, get proof. I've been planning it for ages –' nailing me with her eyes – 'but I need someone to go with me.'

'A collaborator.'

'Exactly!'

'This what you wanted to talk about?'

'Yes, a joint undercover operation. Report back to the ISPCA. What do you say?'

'Well, um . . .'

'I've been waiting ages for someone who cares, someone who knows what I'm talking about, someone whose brain isn't stuffed with Big Macs and football. What do you say?'

Weathering her gaze, joining up her freckles with an imaginary pen. Heart beating, 'Sure, why not? I'm sure I could borrow a camera.'

Rain's arriving like spears on the march, raking the ground, leaping walls, sweeping up the slope to capture us.

Blaise looking at me, hair running with rain, waterfall leaping from her nose. 'You really like the idea?'

Heart twisting and turning, demons going helter-skelter, 'Sure, but it would take some working out.'

'I already worked it out. I wrote to Jack de Barra, calling myself Carmen Santamaria, saying I'm over for a few months learning English, and I believe I've an ancestor buried on the island from the Spanish Armada.'

'Are there Spanish sailors buried there?'

'Yes! Four names in the library, and I picked Fernando Santamaria as my ancestor, and asked de Barra if he'd mind if I paid a visit. Took three letters, and then his secretary rang, said Mr de Barra couldn't see any problem, and to ring him to fix a day! So, how would you like to visit the grave of my imaginary ancestor?'

'An intelligence-gathering operation.'

'You got it! Then we'll have him prosecuted and the animals freed!'

We're running for the house, whooping and laughing. 'Death to Deathrow Dobbs! Freedom for the animals!'

Rain racing ahead of us, Sally and Prudence taking cover in the barn, chicks squeezing under their mother's outspread wings as we splash by.

Peig returns to find us soaked to the skin

and shivering. 'Better get a fire going and find you two some dry clothes.'

Crackling fire matching the rain rattling the window, Blaise coming down in a pair of my jeans rolled up at the ankles, and the only sweatshirt Peig could find without an offending designer label.

'Great place, Mrs Lynch.'

'Glad you like it, but call me Peig if you want to come again.'

'Have you always taken in strays and ill-treated animals . . . Peig?'

'Ever since my parents died,' says Peig, rustling us up some grub.

'Do you ever turn any away?'

'I should, but I don't.'

'In that case, Auntie, we could take in all those poor creatures from Inishbán,' says I, joking of course.

'Which animals, hon?'

'You've not heard about Jethro Dobbs, Peig?' says Blaise. 'And how cruel he is to the animals?'

'That's what people say.'

'Then why doesn't anybody do anything?'

'I did make enquiries once, along with a few others, but somehow he survives the inspections. And Jack de Barra threatens to sue anyone who even breathes the word cruelty.'

'I'm going to get proof, and show the ISPCA.'

'Good for you. But how would you go about it?'

'Get over in disguise and take pictures.'

Peig turns, looks at Blaise. 'And you want Lorcan to come with you, don't you?'

Brandy lets out a bark and ducks into the next room wagging her tail.

'That you, Gabriel?' Peig calling. 'Come on in.'

'Gabriel lives down the road, Blaise,' says I. 'Goes out fishing in the estuary in his boat.'

She nods, not very interested, glancing nervously at Peig.

'He's feeling shy, he'll eat alone,' says Peig, serving up burgers and chips.

Blaise pales. 'I'm real sorry, Mrs Lynch, I don't eat meat.'

'Oh, I never thought –' whisking Blaise's plate away – 'I'll fix you some vegetables from the garden.'

'Oh, please don't go to any—'

Too late. Peig's throwing on a coat and heading out with a knife.

Blaise looking at me, stormy eyebrows. 'I think this mission's in danger.'

'Why?'

'I'm not sure I want to team up with a carnivore. That's dead cow you're about to tuck into!'

'I didn't personally kill it, Blaise.'

167

'No, you let others do your killing for you. If everyone had to shoot cows and slit pigs' throats, there'd be a hell of a lot more vegetarians, I'm telling you.'

Ducking her gaze – I thought Mum was bad!

Peig's back with dripping basket of carrots, cabbage, broad beans and scallions. 'Stir-fry with rice coming up!'

'Thanks, Peig, but there's really no need to—'

'Nonsense, I'm going to join you.'

'Me too please, Auntie.'

'What about your burger, hon?'

'I couldn't possibly –' pushing it away – 'I'm vegetarian.'

Blaise curling up her nose, 'Since when?'

'About three minutes ago.'

Finbar arrives to collect Blaise. Peig insists he joins her for a cuppa. They steam up the kitchen chatting about acupuncture, sculpture and how hard it is to find out anything about the new road.

Blaise whispering, 'Serious planning starts Monday.'

'I'm fighting Clinton Monday.'

'Don't! I need you in one piece.'

'I have to: I'd never be able to hold my head up.'

Time to go, Blaise hesitating before getting

into the car. 'Peig, can Lorcan come with me – to the island?'

Peig turning to Finbar, 'I take it you know about your daughter's mission?'

'I hear nothing else, and it makes me nervous. I'd be a lot happier if she had someone like Lorcan with her.'

Rattly old Saab bumping down the lane, Peig saying, 'I like Blaise – she's got spirit. Attractive too, don't you think?'

'Um – yes. And smart.'

'Oh yes, cute as five hundred pet monkeys, that one.'

Horse neighing in the lane, pushing through the gate. Joseph! Horse and rider looking in the window.

'Goodness, you're popular, and you're only here a week.'

He's remembered the gloves. Training begins with me stalking him round the barn trying to land blows. Now him pursuing me – with a fence post. 'Trust me – Clinton hits you and it'll feel like a lump of wood. Come on . . . Lean, sidestep, duck! Lean, sidestep, duck! And counter-punch, hit back! One-two, one-two – that's it!'

Gasping, quick squirt of inhaler: 'Will I be able to use this during the fight?'

'If it lasts that long.'

Hens wandering in and out, Sadie bounding in for a lick, bounding out again.

'So what is the plan, Joseph? I think I need to know.'

'The plan is this . . .' says he, proceeding to describe a mischievous and very risky strategy.

'Interesting idea, but . . .'

'But what?'

'I don't know if I can do it.'

Joseph chewing hay, wondering the same.

'Mind if I ask you something?'

'What?'

'Why do you keep yourself to yourself at school?'

''Cos I'm a knacker?'

'You're not a knacker – you're a traveller.'

'Yeah, right.'

'Most kids and teachers like you.'

'They'd spit on me if they could.'

'Well, I like you, and I'm one of them.'

'You're not, you're an outsider. You're a dirty Dub and I'm a dirty knacker.'

'Shouldn't say that.'

Laughs. 'I got to go, Lorcan.'

'Train again tomorrow?'

'Can't. Work out on your own. Get yer mind set.'

Following him through the house, the garden, the gate, where Ginny Jo's waiting patiently, nibbling the hedge, 'How do you mean, get my mind set?'

'Stick it in positive mode – *I'm going to*

murder that greaseball – and keep it there. Don't let anything else in.' Vaults up onto Ginny Jo's back and away down the track, kicking up stones.

'Joseph?'

Swings pony round. 'What?'

'What are the chances of your plan working?'

'I wouldn't put money on you.'

'That doesn't make me feel good, Joseph.'

'You'll have to be clever – real clever, and I don't know how clever you are.'

From my window I watch pony and rider vanishing into the rain. Watch the sky breaking up and catching fire. Seems only yesterday I was a Hadley Wood boy doing fine. Now, as if taking on the boy-tyrants of Raven Hill isn't enough, I've gone and said yes to an undercover operation on Inishbán!

It's all too much – *Bring me night, or bring me Blücher!*

Oooh-la-la! Napoleon on fine form *ce soir*, routing the English and trouncing the Prussians, hot elastics singeing Sadie's nose, and somehow she naps through it – amazing!

15

Sunday, church bells on the breeze, phone ringing.

'It's for you, hon!'

Blaise! 'Can you get over here? I got news!'

Hurry! Peig's dropping me off on her way to church. Guiltily wolfing down a plate of eggs and bacon, changing into gear that doesn't flaunt some slave-trading logo, run a squirt of gel through my hair, mess it up a bit so it looks accidentally cool, and run.

Sadie jumping in the back with Brandy, side by side without a word.

Heart beating at the thought of seeing Blaise again, 'Do you mind living alone, Auntie?'

'Not really.'

'Doesn't it get lonely, all this rock and silence?'

'It's a healing solitude, hon.'

'Mind if I ask you something, Auntie?'

'What?'

'Is, um, Dr Sweeney interested?'

Laughs. 'Dr Sweeney? In me?'

'The way he looks at you, you'd think . . .'

'What would you think, hon?'

'He wants to marry you.'

'Ha-ha! What a sweet boy you are.'

Map spread on lap. 'Think it's this turning, Auntie.'

Swing off main road into winding lane rushing to the sea, looking for a plain bungalow with solar panels and a sign saying— There it is! FINBAR MCBRIDE'S CONNEMARA POTTERY.

Peig pulling over, almost into the ditch.

'Thanks, Auntie.'

'Maybe next Sunday you'll accompany me to mass?'

'Definitely – if I'm not in hospital, or jail . . . Only messing.'

Stops me as I'm getting out. 'Let you into a secret. He proposed to me New Year's Eve.'

'What did you say?'

'Said I'd have to consider – and I'm still considering!'

Waving. Then through the gate into a neat front garden crowded with sculptures and glazed pottery. Blaise stretched out in a hammock slung between flowering apple trees, reading a book. Grins, jumps down. 'Quick! Weather's changing.'

She's wearing baggy jeans and a T-shirt saying CARS ARE KILLING CONNEMARA! under a cartoon of a shark-toothed car and manic driver.

'I brought Sadie.'

'Cool! Come on, Sadie, race us!'

Round the side of a kitchen garden tidier than Peig's we run, up a hill to a – *wooh!* – sudden drop to a stony beach ruffled by waves. Before us, across the estuary, Inishbán veiled in haze.

'What's the news?'

'Jack de Barra's secretary called. I'm invited – or rather, Carmen Santamaria is invited – on Saturday. I mentioned you. She left me hanging on ages, and then said that Mr de Barra would have no objection to me bringing a friend. We're going to Inishbán! Here –' handing me binoculars – 'take a look.'

Train them on the southern end of the island . . . grand house and terraced garden. Centre of the island . . . ruined church and cemetery. Up a bit, sheltered by rising ground . . . bungalow and enclosures. Sheep dotted about . . . sea birds wheeling over white cliffs at the northern tip.

'See the sheep's legs?' says Blaise.

'Visibility's not great. They're kind of hopping.'

'That's because he has their back legs tied.'

'Why would he do that?'

'Restricts their movement. Saves on fences.

Wait long enough, and you'll see him kick a donkey or belt a dog.'

'No sign of life in the mansion.'

'The de Barras live mostly on their estate in Kilraine.'

'Bungalow looks quiet too.'

'Lazy bums, Dobbs and Mrs Dobbs.'

'I can see the donkeys . . . and a dog or two.'

'They could be a problem. Them and his guns.'

'Guard dogs and guns?'

'What do you expect, a cocktail reception?'

'You sure TJ's dad doesn't know about the cruelty?'

'I wrote ages ago. He wrote back saying my allegations were slanderous and, like Peig said, he wouldn't hesitate to sue if I repeated them.'

'How we getting there?'

'The ferry. We're invited, remember!'

Wander back to the house. Find Finbar in his cluttered studio chipping away at a sculpture of a naked woman. Sadie licks his hand.

'Hail, son of Ted! How's life in the slow lane?'

'Deadly.'

'You like it here?'

'I do.'

'And are you as sensible as you seem, Lorcan? Because this Operation Snoopy—'

'Snoop – not Snoopy!' protests Blaise.

'– is giving me the heebie-jeebies. Jack de Barra and his gruesome caretaker are not men you'd want to upset.'

'Ah, Da, stop fussing.'

'Maybe you'll put a bit of caution on her, Lorcan?'

'You stick to potting, Da, and we'll stick to plotting,' says Blaise, seizing my hand. 'Come see my room!'

The boring-looking bungalow comes alive inside, living room and kitchen-diner knocked into one spacious, light-filled arena, with big TV and music centre, PC and office tucked into a recess. On the mantelpiece, photos of a smiling woman. Blaise's ma?

'Was your dad always a potter and sculptor?'

'He was an architect. Kind of cracked up after Ma died. Potting and pottering saved his life.'

'And you, I bet.'

Her room's a shock – red walls, purple ceiling, bed an unmade futon and, unlike the rest of the house, it's a mess of clothes flung about; books, files, dirty crockery . . .

'I made Da paint it like this when Ma died. I hate it now. Going to blitz it some day with nice colours.'

'My parents would never let me keep my room this way.'

Laughs. 'I don't let him in to tidy. Look over here: the only thing I'm going to keep – my shout board,' she says, closing a wardrobe to reveal a white board on which she's sketched stoats and badgers and scrawled slogans like EXTINCTION IS FOR EVER! BOY BANDS ARE DIP-STICKS! and MINDS ARE LIKE PARACHUTES, THEY NEED TO BE FULLY OPEN TO WORK and, strangest of all, IS LORCAN DESCENDED FROM HUMANITY DICK?

'What's that supposed to mean?'

'Yonks ago a rich geezer called Richard Martin owned half Connemara. He was always getting into deadly duels – like yours with TJ, only real – and cracking down on tenant farmers who were cruel to their animals. He cared so much he helped set up the RSPCA and people called him Humanity Dick.'

'Blaise, I'm not sure I care as much as you . . .'

'Do you care enough to go under cover with me?'

'I suppose.'

'Suppose isn't good enough. I need commitment.'

'OK, you got it.'

On the window ledge, an assortment of ponies and dolls. 'Don't look at them, they suck.'

'What about these?' Barbie dolls in combat gear, faces smeared with camouflage cream.

'Action Barbie. Customized by yours truly. What kind of music d'you like?'

'Um, U2?'

Rolling her eyes, 'Boring!'

'What do you like?'

'All sorts, Nirvana, Vivaldi, Real World music, especially African stuff like Angelique Kidjo. Bet you never even heard of her.'

'Um, no.'

Clears a path to the CD player and fills the room with a woman's snappy voice and spicy African beat.

'Is that your ma?' Framed photo of pony-tailed woman in judo kit holding a trophy.

'Yes,' handing me an album entitled *Kathy McBride – Ma*: carefully arranged photos of her mum as baby, toddler, schoolgirl, student with cloak and mortarboard, shining bride, new mum with babe in arms, working woman in suit, family shots by the sea . . . on and on until – *oh God!* Could have warned me! Photos and newspaper cuttings: a mangled wreck that was once a car.

Takes the album back, stands it on a shelf. 'Look at this,' she says, spreading a big sheet of paper on the floor, a home-made map of Inishbán. 'I photocopied old maps of the island in the library and made this big one.'

Get down with her to look. Too shocked by the album to take it in.

'Inishbán, the White Island, also known as Lazy Bones, 'cos look –' a photo taken at sea level – 'it looks like someone lying back, hands behind his head – you OK?'

Monday morning, Big Fight Day, looking out the bus window for Joseph, the spot where he always stands – he's not there! Can't see him in the camp site, no sign of him. Heart twisting, breath thinning.

Mocking grin from TJ in class. All through lessons his taunts in my ear: 'Your luck runs out today, Jailchick. Clinty's gonna punch holes in you, send you snivelling home to mammy.'

I long to challenge him about the cruelty on Inishbán, but I can't concentrate on animal welfare and the fight at the same time. Do my best to ignore him; focus instead on Joseph's advice: *Keep your mind set – you're going to thrash that greaseball.*

Clinton staring at me in the playground, and out on the field where I'm playing Gaelic football for the first time, trying to break me mentally before we even get in the ring. Still no sign of Joseph.

'It's not fair –' Blaise protesting loudly – 'boxing's Clinton's thing.'

'Just 'cos you're soft on the Dub,' jeers Courtney.

TJ chuckling, 'Not getting nervous, are we, Jailchick?'

'Nervous? Of fighting Clinton?'

I can only laugh, and they jeer back, because I haven't a hope.

After school a crowd even bigger than before tumbles into the glen.

But not Blaise: 'I don't want to see this.'

'I'll shout for you,' says Little Toad.

'Thanks, Róisín. Could make all the difference.'

Someone's tied lengths of red and white road-workers' ribbon to several wrecked cars to make a crooked boxing ring, placed a blue bucket in one corner, red one in the opposite. Rain's stopped, but the ground's greasy. Maybe Clinton will slip and break his neck. Heart slamming, a lamb before the bullet.

Clinton all puffed up: 'You said you had gloves!'

'My manager's bringing them.'

'You're not ducking out of this, you rat.'

Everyone looking at me. No shame in fighting and losing, but trying to wriggle out of it . . . Shame burning my eyes. Everyone getting restless, ready to go home, giving me sick looks.

What's that? My ears prick up: sound of a pony.

'Look!' Little Toad points. 'It's Sticky Joe!'

On the rise astride Ginny Jo. Beside him, arms folded, Blaise, trying to make up her mind. Joseph's coming, taking his time. If only Blaise would follow – she is, she's coming!

Joseph hops down, pats Ginny Jo on the rump.

TJ unimpressed, 'Where the hell you been?'

My manager gives a laugh, tosses me a pair of shiny shorts with gold trimming, inscribed CARRICKDRUM BOXING CLUB.

'Wow, for me?'

Whoops and whistles from the crowd as we strip to underpants, Clinton pulling shiny blue shorts over massive thighs, mine shiny red over wobbly knees.

'Bare feet,' declares Joseph.

'Says who?' says TJ.

'It's too slippy – it's safer.'

'Suits me,' says Clinton. 'I'll fight him in flippers if you like!'

Edgy laughter all round, girls and boys from our whole year following me with their eyes, wondering how anyone could be mad enough to step into a ring with Clinton – and maybe praying that, by some miracle, I'll punch him clean out of the valley.

This can't be happening. I must be dreaming

one of those dreams where I'm trying desperately to impress Dad.

'See,' Joseph whispers. 'Looks a right git in bare feet.'

He's right. Clinton's big pasty feet make him look like an oversized baby.

Clinton ducks into the ring – jigs, hops, wiggles his muscles to a few cheers, mainly from Courtney. TJ squats on a car bumper, exchanging jokes with his fighter.

Joseph tying my gloves, 'Blaise'll be in your corner.'

'I thought . . .'

'I'm reffing, remember. I gave her the plan.'

The plan – Joseph's crazy plan that might just work, like David's shock win over Goliath.

Joseph dunking a sponge in a puddle; handing it, along with a towel, to Blaise.

Breathing deep and loud, 'Don't expect too much, guys. I mean, look! He's taller, broader and much heavier than me.'

'Yeah, and stupider,' says Blaise.

'Brawn and no brains,' says Joseph. 'Stick to the plan.'

The plan, the plan – the flipping plan.

'And whatever you do, don't get hit!'

'I'll try and remember.'

'Everybody's waiting, Jailchick,' TJ calling.

Climb in, waving to the crowd – cheers, boos, hoots of laughter! They still can't believe it. Only Little Toad going, 'You can do it, Lorcan!'

Joseph clicking his fingers, calling us together, 'This is a five-round contest –' echoing through the valley – 'three minutes each. I'm in charge and I'll stand no monkey business, ye hear? In the blue corner –' introducing my enemy – 'Clinton McNulty, the Beast of Connemara!'

More boos and cheers and Little Toad going, 'Shhhh! Someone will hear!' Wish someone would.

'In the red corner –' introducing me – 'from the back o' beyond, Lorcan Lynch, the Clown of Dublin!' – winks at me.

The plan, the plan – stick to the plan!

'I want a clean fight, ye hear? Now get to your corners, and when you come out, come out fightin'!'

Clinton gives me a lethal look. I smile back and go looking for Blaise's reassuring eyes. She's smiling bravely, scared I'm going to get murdered. 'Best o' luck, Che – he'll never know what hit him!'

You'd think I had a revolver tucked in me shorts!

'Seconds out! Get yer butts out here and fight!'

Head horribly clear, legs like water. Clinton's all jizzed up, eyes so focused you'd swear he'd been waiting all his life for this

183

moment. Here he comes, real professional, swaying on his hips, peering at me over his gloves. Why? What's he think I'm going to do – hit him? Round and round we circle, eyeing each other, Clinton's stare full of spite and menace, mine stupid as I can make it. He's all meat and bounce – me a quivering jellyfish.

He throws a punch – *duck* – flies over. Jabs – *lean left*; jabs again – *lean right*; swings with the right – *jump clear*. Crowd applauds – 'Yeh!' – doing fine.

Keeping his guard up, staring at me, wondering why he still hasn't hit me when I look so stupid. He's getting mad, picking up the pace – and now for the tricky bit, surviving the rest of the round with him charging and spraying punches, and me bobbing and weaving and finally skipping away like a rabbit, round and round the ring with him chasing and flinging punches – the crowd loving it, and me spinning and whirling and *bang!* – that's it, I'm finished, knees and forehead on moss and stone.

'One – two – three . . .'

Joseph in my ear, 'Get up, Lorcan, get up!'

Applause! Boos! Courtney's thrilling voice, 'Nice one, Clinty!'

I'm up. Joseph's in my face murmuring, 'Thirty seconds.'

TJ yelling, 'Come on, get on with it!'

Clinton on the rampage again, me into my

184

rabbit dance, twisting this way and that, dodging punches as they fly like grapeshot, missing, glancing, battering my gloves until – '*Ouch!*' Not a punch; a sharp stone underfoot, and I'm hopping like an eejit and *bang!* Clinton's fist propels me into the corner, where someone – Blaise! – catches me. 'That's enough – leave him alone!'

Bang! Bang! Two big hits to the head and I go down like a puppet, strings severed, cheek to stone.

'One – two – three . . .'

TJ boiling over, 'You're calling too slow!'

'Four – five . . . back to your corner, McNulty!'

'Too slow, you cheat!'

'Shut it, de Barra, or your man's disqualified.'

'You can't do that!'

'Wanna bet? Six – seven . . . Come on, Lorcan, for Jeez' sake!'

I'm up, eyes watering, whole valley lurching like a ship – Clinton trying to get at me, Joseph blocking him, clapping his hands. 'Get back! End of round one! You deaf? Get back!'

Mighty sigh from Joseph. You'd think *he'd* survived the round.

Sink onto upturned bucket – cold sponge in the face. 'Inhaler, quick! How'm I doing?'

'How's he doing?' Blaise putting the inhaler to my lips.

'Grand. Got him just where you want him.'

'I have?' – licking blood.

'He thinks you're finished.'

'You mean I'm not?'

'He's all set up, sitting duck. He's yours!'

'Come on, Sticky, time's up!' TJ banging his watch.

Joseph's breath on my brow. 'This is it, pal – play dead a teeny bit more and then . . .' His eyes say the rest.

He's counting on me; so is Dad, so is Mum in her way, and the brother or sister I lost each time Mum miscarried – I want to win this for them, and for Blaise, and all the persecuted kids in class like Hedgehog Thomas and Little Toad, and all the miserable animals on Inishbán – this one's for you too . . .

Head throbbing, cheeks burning, I'm on my feet, shoulders down like a beaten dog, Clinton closing in, licking his lips like he hasn't eaten for a month and I'm his dinner – so sure, his hands hang loose. He could *blow* me over! And here he comes, big ugly face and sweaty neck, sauntering with a sad little smile, like, *Sorry to have to do this, but – BANG! –*

Only that wasn't him this time, that was me, straight in his face, eyes nearly hopping out of their sockets with surprise, and then – rest of the plan! – almighty swing to the belly, so hard my gloved fist buries itself in guts –

nearly comes out of his back! And another! And another! Same spot, making him double over and groan like a drunk about to puke, his face thrown forward so all I need do is remove my fist from his belly and jab hard up into his chin, throwing his head up straight again, gaping! Because it's not a frightened fool he's fighting now, it's a mad thing with bared teeth and eyes blazing – swinging like a lunatic, pummelling his face – *bang-bang!* Fast as I can – *bang-bang-bang!* – so even if the punches aren't that hard, they're too quick to block, until at last, when I've nearly nothing left, he drops to his knees like a rhino, sinks to the stones and lies still, mouth open, nose running red.

Stunned silence fills the valley. Joseph leaps at me, seizes my wrist, thrusts it skyward. 'The winner – the undisputed champion of Raven Hill – Lorcan *the Clown* Lynch!'

The crowd roars! Roars! *ROARS!*

TJ, looking decidedly uncomfortable, helping his man to his knees.

Clown collapsing, fighting for air. It's not an attack, just a little over-exertion. Someone's arms around me – Blaise!

Face puffy, muscles aching. Peig looking at me closely, listening to my breathing, 'I'm shocked you didn't tell me,' dabbing round my eyes with stinging lotion.

187

'It's OK, Auntie, he won't come near again.'

Leading me into her practice, helping me off with my shirt, coming at me with a packet of long, white-tipped needles. They go in rapidly, like flag pins in a board, into my chest, elbow and collar bone – *ouch, ouch, ouch*. Actually, they don't hurt. Only here and there a little after-sting, like a puppy's nip.

Sleep the sleep of the giant-slayer.

17

Someone gently shaking me. 'Wake up, hon, you're running late.'

Surfacing from the deep. Where am I? Peig's house, Che Guevara's bed. What day is it? Heart beating horribly, nearly leaping out of my chest with fear – the thought of facing Clinton . . .

Wait! It's Tuesday! It's over: Joseph's plan worked. The Clown played dumb and blitzed the Beast. I won! I pursued the impossible – and won. Relief washes over me. Everything hurts, and I don't care, lifting myself limb by limb out of bed. Feels as if a hundred-year-old man swapped joints with me in the night.

Glorious food, gallons of water, Sadie's woolly head. 'You getting to feel at home, girl?'

Sadie lazily flapping her tail.

Riding the bus in a daze, every bump hurts, and makes me smile. Hedgehog Thomas next to me going, 'It was so great! The way he came at you, hands down and laughing, the big-head! And then, *bam!* Between the eyes! *Bam-bam-bam!'* demonstrating on the back of the seat in front. 'I loved it, Lorcan – loved it!'

There's Joseph, leaping puddles through the encampment.

On my feet – 'Hang on, please, driver!'

Joseph bounding aboard, bouncing into a seat across from us. 'Feeling sore?'

'Just a bit.'

Laughing – happier than I've ever seen him.

'It was brilliant, Sticky— I mean Joseph!' blurts Thomas. 'Never forget it long as I live.'

Joseph gives him half a smile.

No sign of Clinton in school. Kids in corridors grinning at me, giving me thumbs up. Little Toad skipping into class, giggling, bursting out of herself – 'I couldn't sleep last night, I was so happy remembering the way you looked finished and then came back and wasted him – and the faces on TJ and Courtney – should have seen them!'

Courtney, sitting on her desk fooling with her mobile, looks up, scowls. 'What was that, Fatso?'

'Don't call me that!'

'Ah, shuddup.'

'No, *you* shuddup!' snaps Róisín. 'I'm sick of you calling me names.'

Cheers all round - 'You tell her, Róisín!'

190

Courtney flicks her hair back, cool as a pop star, but her cheeks are hot, and there's a new mood in the room: everything feels cool and light. The bullies have been whipped and everyone's acting silly – apart from TJ and Courtney, who look like a pair of stuffed owls.

Still no sign of Clinton. Slide in next to TJ.

'Morning, TJ.'

'You look terrible, Jailchick.'

'I feel fine, Buzzy.'

'You made hard work of it.'

'I beat him.'

'Clint's a big softie. Anyone could beat him.'

'Well, that was cruel of me then, wasn't it?'

'What you talking about?'

'And talking of cruelty, what's all this about animals mistreated on Inishbán?'

Quick as a flash – 'Who told you that?'

'Everybody.'

'You mean that rat Blaise.'

'I mean everybody. They all say your da's caretaker beats, kicks and starves the animals half to death.'

'Well, it's all lies, and he'll sue anyone – and I mean *anyone* –' jabbing a finger in my face – 'who dares repeat them.

Miss Maddigan calling our names, stops at mine: 'You all right today, Che Guevara?'

'Fine, thanks, miss.'

'I so enjoyed your talk. All weekend I was

thinking about Che Guevara dining and dancing with your family.'

Door swings wide – enter Clinton puffy-eyed, school bag slung over shoulder, bold as brass.

'Don't we knock any more, Mr McNulty?'

Making a big show of going back out, fisting the door and breezing in like he just won the world title with one hand tied. Leans back on his chair, grinning like a fool. No one's smiling back. Keeps looking this way, but even TJ's ignoring him.

Miss Maddigan returning our Irish compositions: 'Róisín, excellent. Blaise, good. TJ, erratic as usual. Lorcan – your Spanish is promising, but your Irish is a disaster!'

Knock-knock: enter a tall, stern senior boy, 'Excuse me, miss, Mr Trench wants Clinton and Lorcan outside his door.'

Murmurs round the room, Miss Maddigan peering over her specs.

Walking together in silence, shoulder to shoulder down gloomy corridors. Standing either side of Mr Trench's door, Clinton looking anxious. Suddenly says, 'Some swine must have snitched. I'll kill him.'

Door flies open – Mr Trench waving us in like a traffic cop, face full of rage. 'Stand up straight, the pair of you.' Turning to me, eyes blazing, '*Missster* Lynch, you surprise me. I allowed you into my school on the understanding you caused no trouble. You're only here a week and throwing your weight around already. What have you to say?'

Heart hammering, 'I'm sorry, sir, it wasn't my intention to cause—'

'Well, you have, and you picked the wrong boy when you attacked Clinton. His father is our TD and an important member of the community.'

Phone going. Snatches it up – 'Yes? . . . Put her through . . . Mrs McNulty, forgive me, they've just arrived, so if you wouldn't mind calling back in a couple of . . . Thank you so much.' Hanging up, glaring at me, 'What have you to say for yourself?'

'I didn't exactly attack him, sir.'

'I'll have no lies, young man.'

'And we were wearing gloves.'

'Gloves? What do you mean gloves?'

I'm looking at Clinton; he's looking away. 'We were boxing, sir.'

'Boxing? Mrs McNulty says it was an unprovoked assault after school.'

'It was after school, but it was a contest, sir – five rounds, three minutes each.'

'Where did this so-called boxing match occur?'

'Devil's Glen.'

Switching his glare to Clinton, 'A boxing contest, Master McNulty . . . What do we know about that?'

Phone again. 'Yes, Mrs McNulty, we seem to have two versions. Young Lynch claims it was a boxing match, with gloves . . . Just a moment.' Squinting at me, 'You wouldn't happen to have any witnesses?'

'TJ de Barra in Clinton's corner, Blaise McBride in mine, Joseph Tully the referee and about thirty spectators from our year.'

'Is this true, Clinton?'

'Well, I'm not sure there were that many.'

Thrusting the phone at Clinton, 'Perhaps you better have a word.' Clinton shaking as he takes the call.

Mr Trench returning to me, 'What on earth induced you to indulge in boxing without proper supervision? I want an absolute assurance that the remainder of your time in my school will be entirely without incident.'

Suddenly back in court, the judge glaring at Dad: *Are you willing to reassure the court that under no circumstances will you re-engage in such reprehensible behaviour?*

'I'll do my best, sir . . .'

'You certainly will, young man,' says Mr Trench, taking back the phone. 'Mrs McNulty, I'm sorry about all this, and I can assure you . . . Yes, of course, I absolutely agree . . . Thank you so much. Goodbye.'

Throws open the door. 'I ought to suspend the pair of you, but the good name of the school comes first. Come with me.'

Marched back to class like criminals.

'Miss Maddigan, I want see the entire year in the hall immediately!'

Sitting on the hall floor, heads up, backs straight. Mr Trench pacing like a thundercloud.

'Not a word of this appalling episode will leave the school gate. The last thing we want is people hearing rumours about goings-on in the glen after school. You will not discuss it amongst yourselves, or with your families – *is that understood?*'

Returning to class, Clinton acts cool, Jack the lad. 'Silly old fool!' he's laughing. 'Ma gave him a right roasting.'

'Listen here, Clinton,' pulling him back by the sleeve.

'What?'

Eye to eye in crowded corridor: 'You lied. You said I attacked you. You could have got me in serious trouble.'

'Relax, Lorcan, we didn't get suspended.'

'Don't you call me Lorcan – it's *Jailchick*, right? And don't you forget it!'

PART THREE

RAIDERS OF THE LONG NIGHT

Strong light in the window, clock says nearly seven. Lie back and drift – no newspapers crashing through the letter box below to disturb me.

Eek-eek! Freddie the fearless pheasant! Fling back curtains, Sadie and I looking out together. Freddie on the sparkling lawn – more a wild-flowering meadow dusted with apple blossom – tossing bits of currant bun like an Olympic event.

Breakfast over, Peig showing me into her practice, where two early patients are waiting – an old lady with arthritis and a young farmer with a bad hip. Peig wearing a white coat looks official and formal, but chats with her patients like old pals. Each disappears behind a curtain and I wait my turn. It's my third time, and I'm still nervous of the needles.

Sadie wandering in, sniffing around. 'Not sure you're allowed,' says I. Grunts and wanders out again.

My turn. Peig sitting me in a cubicle with my shirt off, popping two, three – nine needles in my elbow, chest and collarbone in quick succession. Brace myself once again – *ouch, ouch, ouch!* – but hardly feel them, fleeting electrical pulses, butterfly stings.

Sadie putting her head in, looking at me strangely. 'It's OK, Sadie, they don't hurt!'

Peig leaves me to sit reading a book. I wouldn't know there were any needles in me until I move a limb, and then they twinge. Glancing in the mirror, I look like Gulliver after an attack by Lilliputian bowmen.

Haven't used my inhaler since the fight. Is it pure chance or the needles that I'm breathing better? Or cleaner air? Or because everything's cool in school: new mood in class, kids talking and laughing who were quiet before. Even Joseph's loosening up.

Waiting for the bus, peaceful after the needles, wondering whether my demons are really beginning to lose their power over me. Breathing in purple mountains and endless sky, bright blue here, feathery white over there, grey over Kilraine and thundery black on the horizon – four skies in one. Sit on the grass verge watching a couple of red beetles mating on a leaf.

The bus!

Bouncing along, watching the fields go by,

each one different, no two things in nature the same.

Joseph hops aboard, flops next me.

'Hi, Joseph.'

Yawning, flexing his fingers, 'Call me Joey, if you want.' Says it real casual, but I think it means we're officially friends.

In the playground at break, a shock. Little Toad whispering, 'Could you do with help on the island?'

'What?'

'When you and Blaise go over and—'

'Who says we're going over?'

'Couldn't help overhearing.'

'You must have bats' ears, Róisín!' says I, too rough.

'Sorry,' lowering her eyes.

Just wounded my most loyal fan.

'Have you said anything to anyone?'

'No, 'course not.'

'You quite sure?'

'Who'd listen to me?'

'All right then, but don't tell Blaise you know. We're going over secretly to gather evidence of cruelty.'

'Can I come?'

'I don't think so. But, um, maybe next time.'

Noon in the little fishing port of Rialto, Operation Snoop about to get underway – strolling along the pier, pulses racing. Wild

201

and beautiful down here, rocky shoreline and choppy water, breeze straight in from America.

Blaise, suddenly, 'Did you remember your aunt's camera?'

'Sure,' says I, cool as you like, when inside I'm a hive of nerves.

Blaise, in her best Spanish accent – which sounds more like French to me – is getting herself in a fight with the ferryman, lanky feller in long boots and Aran jumper.

'But I'm telling you, I no have my puzzer-port wiz me.'

'Sorry, miss – no ID, no go.'

'Then please explain ziz to Señor de Barra, when we no arrive for lernch.'

'Saints preserve us!' whipping out a mobile and walking away.

'Fingers crossed,' murmurs Blaise.

Decided to dress up – Peig's idea – so I'm in the suit and shirt Mum insisted on packing, and Blaise looks elegant in mauve linen jacket and pleated skirt with shoulder bag, hair tied back, dark glasses, eyelids shaded mauve, lips smeared with pale pink lipstick. Looks at least sixteen.

'What are you laughing at?'

'Sorry, but you look so . . . different.'

'It's Carmen, not me – OK?'

Ferryman's back. 'What's your name?'

'Carmen Santamaria.'

'Right, you're on!'

Car pulling up, woman – heavy like Mum getting out with a red leather briefcase, hurrying over waving her ID.

'I know her,' says Blaise, suddenly pale.

'Who is she?'

'She won't recognize me.'

The woman Blaise knows better be careful, because the boat's tipping and greasy underfoot as she steps down and – just as I expected – slips! Quick! Both of us leaping to catch her.

Holding her heart, 'Thank you so much. Angels, the pair of you!'

Blaise retrieving the red briefcase, wiping it down, 'Forgot your name, but I remember you from the hairdresser's in Kilraine.'

'I'm Marie and I work for myself now, visiting people at home.'

Blaise looking troubled as the boat heaves out into the stream, and the pier slides away. 'You used to do my ma's hair.'

'Really, who . . . ?'

'Kathy McBride.'

'Oh my dear, I'm so sorry. You must be – let me see – Blaise. She was a lovely woman, your ma. Talked about you non-stop.'

Blaise looks away, eyes shining in the glare.

'Are you going over to cut someone's hair?' says I, making conversation.

'Mrs de Barra's. What about you? And why are we whispering?'

Blaise hesitating, 'I'm supposed to be Spanish . . .'

'Spanish?'

'We're undercover.'

'How intriguing!'

'Can you keep a secret?' Blaise whispering urgently.

'Yes, I think so.'

'Have you heard about the animals on Inishbán being ill-treated?'

'Rumours, yes, but—?'

'I've been watching the island through binoculars for seventeen months, and five days, watching the caretaker, Jethro Dobbs, kicking and starving the animals. We're looking for proof, so that we can say, *Listen, something's got to be done about this!*'

'Does Mr de Barra know about the cruelty?'

'We think so, but he threatens to prosecute anyone who mentions it.'

'Well, between you and me –' whispering so low in the breeze, we have to lean in close to hear – 'Jack de Barra's not a kind man, and I'd be very careful if I were you.'

Listening to this, I'm scared. This isn't a game: it's happening, we're sailing to someone's island to snoop around and accuse them of cruelty. Heart beating faster, breath coming quicker, wishing I was back at Peig's firing elastics.

Tipping and lifting in the swirling water,

sprayed by sea and blinded by sun. Straight ahead, reclining in the mist, Lazy Bones waiting to leap up and tear us to bits.

'Why Spanish?' whispers Marie.

'He knows me, I've written angry letters, so I picked a new identity, with an ancestor buried in the cemetery, and they've agreed to a visit. Marie, could you help us?'

'Help? How?'

'Warn us of danger – like, if you see TJ, their son. He's in our class and would recognize us.'

Marie shaking her head in wonder, 'What a pleasure to meet two such daring young people.'

Estuary racing inland from the open sea, pools of swirling overlapping water. Blaise violently nudging me, 'Did you remember the dog chews?'

'What . . . ?' patting my pockets.

'Don't tell me . . .'

'I got them!' *Phew!*

Ferry pitching in the swell, swinging south of the island and throttling down in an angry roar to thrash a way into a wide cove, a jetty rocking side to side, made of rubber blocks. Car waiting, flustered woman at the wheel.

'Mrs Gleeson, the housekeeper,' Marie informs us.

Ferryman helps us all off.

'You're late! Mrs de Barra's waiting!' flaps Mrs Gleeson, ushering Marie into the car.

'Oh, I am sorry,' Marie replies, winking at us as if to say, *It's hardly my fault.* 'Could we give these two young people a lift?'

'I think we're late enough already, don't you?'

'We'll walk,' says Blaise.

Marie gives us a furtive thumbs up for luck and drives off with Mrs Gleeson. Blaise looks at me, flushed with excitement. 'The spies have landed!'

'Yes!' says I, worried I might succumb to an attack, let Blaise down and make a fool of myself.

Taking the lodge road, wind in our faces, belly heaving with nerves. Clarendon Lodge looming round a bend, majestic ancient mansion cloaked in ivy. Clashing with its elegance and stone, a helipad slapped down on rock and heather, helicopter gleaming in the sun with J. DE BARRA – GALAXY HOLDINGS emblazoned on the side. Dad's mortal foe.

Heart beating wildly – *Dad, you'll never guess!* Sudden thought: 'What if someone here speaks Spanish?'

'Don't, please.'

'What if TJ's here?'

'Just pray he isn't!'

Climbing steps to a porch, massive wooden door and thick stone walls built to defy the

206

worst of winter; old brass bell *ding-dong*ing through the house.

'Remember, Lorcan, I'm Carmen and you're – Damn! We didn't give you a name!'

Footsteps, door flung wide – stone-faced Mrs Gleeson in an apron. 'And you are . . . ?'

'Carmen Santamaria, and zis is my friend, um – Che.'

'Wait here.'

'Che,' says I. 'I like it.'

'Then you better live up to it.'

'Sure?' says I, feeling as if someone has just draped a powerful cloak around my shoulders.

Inside we hear Mrs Gleeson calling politely, 'Mrs de Barra? It's the Spanish girl.' Returning, harsh again, 'Come in.'

Stepping through a broad vestibule into a grand hall hung with drapes and gaudy chandeliers. Men's voices in a room nearby: 'Good work, Jack! Let's drink to it.'

'To progress, prosperity and – discretion!'

I can see Blaise is listening – intently.

'You wanted to see the graveyard?' A woman's voice.

Look up. It's Mrs de Barra leaning over the banister of a gallery, sunglasses in hand. Marie's with her, red briefcase at the ready.

'Yes, eef you please.'

'Those are the children I was telling you about –' Marie addressing Mrs de Barra –

207

'who came to my aid when I slipped.'

'Ah yes. Mrs Gleeson, will you show them the way? I'll call Mr Dobbs, tell him to meet them.'

'They might get to meet your son TJ, Mrs de Barra,' says Marie, 'and his friend – what was his name?'

Blaise and I exchanging glances.

'Clinton,' says Mrs de Barra, never guessing that Marie's innocent little remark is a warning to us.

'Follow me,' says Mrs Gleeson, marching down the hall and knocking at an open door. 'Excuse me, Mr de Barra – the Spanish girl. Shall I—?'

'Yes, show her through.'

Ushered through a lavish living room, where away to one side, in a raised dining area, four men in summer suits are poring over sheets of paper spread on a bare dining table. Recognize two of the men at once – Jack de Barra and Willie-John McNulty.

'And the beauty of this route,' one of the men is saying, 'is that there shouldn't be too much compensation to shell out.'

'On the other hand,' says another, 'it'll stir up a whole hornets' nest of environmentalists.'

Blaise glancing at me wide-eyed. Anxious to hear more, she drops her bag at the open French windows, spilling some of its contents.

Mrs Gleeson turning impatiently, Blaise and I getting in each other's way picking up her belongings.

'We just need to keep the plans quiet, leave objectors as little time as possible to react.'

'Then rapid construction will be down to you, Jack.'

'And some smooth PR work down to Willie-John and the rest of you.'

'Come on, we'll be here all day,' snaps Mrs Gleeson.

'I'm zo zorry,' says Blaise, and we follow the housekeeper onto a garden terrace, where an old lady is sunning herself – 'TJ's gran,' whispers Blaise – and a girl about sixteen is reading a magazine, feet up on a chair – 'TJ's sister Nicole' – both ignoring us.

Down the garden steps to a mossy track Mrs Gleeson leads us and stops. 'Keep to the path and Mr Dobbs will meet you.'

'Zank you zo much.'

She's gone. Blaise can barely contain herself: 'I'm here, I'm really here! All those days and months spying on Deathrow Dobbs and I'm going to meet him any second! And those plans –' grabbing my arm – 'that's the new road! Your aunt and my da would kill to see them. We've got to take a peek before we leave! Did you hear? They want keep the route secret till it's too late to stop it.'

'*Shhh!* You heard Marie –' my turn to grab

Blaise's arm – 'TJ and Clinton are here somewhere.'

'I forgot!'

'You look that way, I'll look this.'

Proceeding cautiously now, eyes peeled. Track dipping to the flat belly of the island – rock, grass and nibbling sheep.

'No sign of Dobbs,' says Blaise, aiming her binoculars ahead. 'Take a look at the sheep.'

Hands me the binoculars and I pick out several sheep clustered on the hillside. 'Blaise, their legs aren't tied! Look – none of them. You sure you didn't make a mistake?'

'Mistake? I've been watching the island for seventeen months and—'

'I know, I know.'

The sheep haven't seen us. The nearest one is a stone's throw away, half hidden by scrub and boulder.

'I'll keep watch. Go get a closer look,' says Blaise, and I move off, head down and not stopping, because Che Guevara wrote in his guerrilla manual that continuous movement draws less attention than stop-go. Crouching close to a ewe, who's a mess of mangled lumpy wool on spindly legs. These are the filthiest sheep I've ever seen, and Blaise is right – look at the red burn marks on the legs. Reaching carefully for my camera, crawl closer, aim, *click – click – click*.

Ewe looks round, takes off in a stumbling

panic, sparking alarm all over the slopes: sheep and lambs waddling away fast as they can under the weight of their filthy coats. And one of them is staggering, and no wonder – its feet are tied.

Run back to tell Blaise, 'You're right, their legs are raw, and one of them is still tied.'

'Must have untied them when he heard we were coming.'

'All the work we've put him to,' says I, dreading meeting the ogre. 'He won't like us much for that.'

'Talk of the devil,' murmurs Blaise.

Grisly-looking character in wellies, shuffling towards us tearing a chicken leg with his teeth.

Blaise freezes, face to face with *her* mortal foe. He doesn't even look at us, just points to a barely visible path.

'I hop you weren't disturbed having your lernch?'

Grunts, 'What?'

'We hop we didn't disturb your lernch, Meestair Dobb?'

'Name's Dobbs – and yes, you did.'

'Oh, I am sorree.'

'Anycase, don't know what y'expect to find.'

'Ze grev of my ancestor, who ran aground in feefteen eighty-eight.'

'Well, if he's here, there'll not be much left of him.'

Never met such a revolting individual: less physically ugly than Gabriel, but more repulsive, fleshy red face and piggy eyes, filthy nails, grubby trousers and jumper, belly bulging over a thick belt – and, worst of all, an evil air about him, like he might be capable of anything: stalking schoolkids, eating babies.

Rough path twisting down to ruined shell of a church. Cemetery's in bits, dozens of broken headstones sticking out like teeth.

'Are they all sailors, Mr Dobbs?' I'm wondering.

'No, the foreigners are over there,' pointing away to four lonely headstones.

'So a lot of people must have lived here once?'

'Couldn't tell you.'

'It's a mess!' blurts Blaise.

Glance at her in horror. She's forgotten her accent.

Dobbs glaring, 'Whazzat?'

'I said it iz a pity for dead peepoll to end up all crooked like zis.'

'I look after it best I can, but it fell into disrepute years ago.' Flings his chicken bone away and leaves us.

Blaise watches him go. 'Imagine employing a caretaker like that. You wouldn't leave a rag doll in his care, never mind an animal.'

'I'd put him to work in the sewers,' says I.

'What, inflict him on the rats?' says she and we're laughing, hard as we can, to wash the taste of Jethro Dobbs out of our mouths. 'Anyway, he shoots rats. You should see him, stumbling around drunk. Keep wishing he'd shoot himself.'

'Do we really need to visit his house?'

'Yes! We've got to see the evidence up close, and get a few snaps if we can,' says Blaise, scanning the island through binoculars, while I examine the Spanish graves, looking for a Santamaria. Centuries of rain, wind and salt have scrubbed the headstones, so it's hard to decipher the names of the dead.

'Lorcan!'

'What?'

'It's them!'

Chucks me the binoculars. Train them down the slope towards the sea, and there they are, TJ and Clinton fishing with their backs to us. Close by, a tent.

'Let's go!' says Blaise.

Scrambling back to the track, on towards Dobbs's place. Pong of burning plastic on the breeze. Round a rocky bend thick with gorse – and there it is, hundred metres off, the outline of a house, wreathed in smoke.

Approaching carefully, cameras at the ready. 'Look!'

Off the track, in a scruffy enclosure well short of the house, the two donkeys and the piebald pony Blaise has been watching for so long, standing motionless. We move closer and see how desperately weak and thin they look, ribs sticking out, scabby coats, hooves overgrown, all three heads hanging as though they lack the strength to lift them. Their big animal eyes, swarming with flies, follow us as we take pictures.

A movement in the corner of my eye: someone emerging from the back of the house. Nudge Blaise –

Woman in shabby dress and cardigan,

cigarette in mouth, moves unsteadily towards a washing line. Smoke changes direction again, obscuring her. Quick, more pictures!

Smoke clears. Woman pinning sheets on the line, working clumsily on wobbly legs, cigarette hanging.

Whispering, 'Can she really be drunk at this time of day?'

'Yes!'

Slowly approaching the house.

The smoke, coming from a rubbish tip, shifts to reveal an old stone bungalow, with new roof and double glazing. Not a pretty sight. The dirty windows are closed in this gorgeous weather, and there's litter strewn across the garden, caught in shrubs and on barbed-wire fences. Outside the back door two huge tractor tyres overflow with empty bottles. In the far corner of the garden the smouldering tip: a mound of ash topped with burned-out mattresses, a charred toilet seat, blackened fridge with its guts hanging out. And look! – Blaise nudging me – a long, muscular-looking rat exploring the edges of the heap, whiskers twitching.

Inside the garden fence two mangy sheep-dogs doze in the sun, one young, one old. Third dog, a scraggy little mongrel, lies like a half-dead thing, too weak to chase the flies from its face. Their homes three rusty oil drums lying on their sides. Outside each, a nearly empty dish of filthy water. Flies gather round dog faeces in the grass. Flies everywhere. Exchanging looks with Blaise: such a desolate scene, hardly a sound or movement, only the younger sheepdog scratching itself raw, and the little mongrel rubbing its runny, swarming eyes. They haven't seen or smelled us yet. Not expecting visitors.

At one side of the house, in a caged pen, scruffy hens peck lethargically. In the adjoining pen, half a dozen plump ducks sit around bored.

Woman turns, stiffens. She's thin and pale, sickly looking. Give her a friendly wave. Staring back at us, hawk eyes in pinched face, 'Dobbs!'

Raa-raa-raa! Young dog leaping up, or trying to; legs too puny to match his will. Stumbling towards us – *raa-raa-raa!* – checked by the barbed fence. Old dog trying to rise, barking feebly.

Dobbs appears at the front door, squinty-eyed in the drifting smoke. Sees us, gapes, 'What d'you want now?' Can't hear us over the din. Cursing and coming over, 'Shuddup, dog!' Dog flinches, tail between legs. 'What do you mean by coming round here?'

'Sorry, Mr Dobbs . . .' says I.

'And what do you want with them cameras?'

'The island's so beautiful and—'

'Didn't you get what you came for?'

216

'Yes, but we wanted to take some pictures of the lovely—'

'You've no business taking pictures. This is private property!'

'Nice dog!' Blaise squatting down, younger sheepdog snarling through wire.

'Shuddup, ye stupid animal!' roars Dobbs, twisting his collar-chain, choking him.

Blaise signalling to me, 'A chew, quick!'

Old dog limping over, barking flimsily.

Blaise: 'Is ze old one ze muzzer?'

'I suppose, but you're upsetting them, move back, get away, go on!'

'What are zair names? Such nice dogs.'

'Dog and dog – what else would I call them? Now get going.'

Blaise reaching to open the gate, 'Here, dog, I have somezing for you.'

'Hey! What do you think you're—?'

Pushing her way in, 'Here, dog, good dog . . .' – even paler than the day she gave her talk.

'Are you cracked? Who said you could—?'

'Is OK, eere, 'ave one of zeese!' And then to me, in mime, *Get in here!*

What?

In!

Old dog barking in confusion, young dog going mad, Dobbs yanking him back, 'Get out, you stupid girl, can't you see you're upsetting them?'

Here goes! Going in and offering old dog a chew.

'What the hell . . . ?' Dobbs hollers at me. 'Didn't I just tell her to get out?'

'Here, old mamma dog, have a chew,' says I, scared of the old dog's teeth, scareder still of Dobbs.

'You stone flaming deaf? Get out, the pair of ye!'

'Iz no problem, Meestair Dobbs, please let him go.'

'Let him go? He'll bite ye legs off.'

'Is OK, dogs don't bite me.'

Old dog sniffing me, picking up the scent of Sadie and Brandy.

'You asked for it, as God's me witness,' says Dobbs, releasing the dog, who lurches forward barking at Blaise, at me, Blaise again – snapping round our knees.

Following Blaise's lead, stand perfectly still, one hand offering a chew, the other behind my back. Dog stops barking. Drooling now, sniffing the chew, sticky-out ribcage swelling like an accordion.

'What the divil d'you two want?' cries Mrs Dobbs, voice slurred and legs jerky with drink.

'Oh hello!' says I. 'We really like your dogs.'

'I told them to keep out,' says Dobbs, 'and what do you they do? March right in and start feeding the dogs, like a flamin' zoo!'

218

'Go on, old girl, try one,' says I, chew trembling in hand. Old dog takes it! Creeps off into her oil drum.

'Never mind that it's *my* property,' goes Dobbs, '*my* dogs. Go ahead, don't let me stop you!' – laughing now, throwing nervous glances at his wife, who also looks capable of anything: evil spells, torture, murder; wide creepy eyes staring at us out of a papery face, skin yellow, mouth black with bad teeth.

'Typical foreigners!' she's saying. 'Think they can come over here and do as they please – well, you can take yerselves off, you and your fancy airs.'

'Taking pictures, they were,' says Dobbs.

'Pictures?' Mrs Dobbs's eyes narrowing with suspicion. 'They've no business taking pictures. Send them away!' she says, weaving her way back indoors.

Young dog sniffing my trousers with interest, jumps back expecting to be hit. Approaches Blaise again, stretching his neck towards the outstretched chew. Even Dobbs is curious to see: will he? Yes! Takes it in his teeth, stumbles off with it.

'Raving mad, the pair of you,' says Dobbs, scratching his belly, holding the gate open for us to leave.

I can't wait, but Blaise isn't ready. She's going over to the little mongrel, bending to stroke it. It flinches, she murmurs soft words, spits on a hankie and wipes its eyes.

'I don't believe this,' Dobbs combing fingers through his thin, greasy hair.

'Why your dogs so zin, Meestair Dobbs?'

'Whazzat?'

'I never seen dogs so zin.'

'*Thin?* They're spoilt rotten, the lot of them.'

'I zink you don't give zem enough to eat.'

Pebbly eyes bulging, 'Cheeky brat! Who d'you think you are, coming in here—?'

'Eef you keep animals, you must care for zem.'

Trudging across and leaning over her, ''Tis none of yer business, you interfering little—' Nearly grabs hold of her – thinks better of it. 'Be off with you, you little scut! You an' all,' grabbing me by the arm and shoving me through the gate. 'Nosy scumbags, I'll put manners on ye!'

Holding the gate for Blaise, but she's still tending the mongrel. '*GET OUT!* Or I'll fetch Mr de Barra.'

Placing a chew between the little mongrel's paws, Blaise rises slowly, looks Dobbs in the eye as she leaves. Securing the gate after her, Dobbs turns his head and shoots a gob of spit onto the grass. If only I was brave as my dad, I'd knock him down with a single punch, and warn him never to go near a living animal again.

'Keep walking, and don't stop till you're off

the island!' he bawls after us. 'And don't show your faces again, ye hear!'

Walking in silence, past the wretched donkeys and pony, down to the rocky bend, where Blaise, eyes brilliant with tears, stops to look back.

'We didn't get the dogs.'

Dobbs watching us. Can't see the little mongrel, but the sheepdogs are just visible, gnawing their chews.

'Not a single picture.'

'We could always come back,' says I, shaking uncontrollably, because I've never experienced such a horrible confrontation.

'Oh yeah, with what excuse this time?'

'Wouldn't need an excuse,' says I. 'Gabriel could bring us.'

'Gabriel?'

'I told you – he has a boat.'

'You think he'd bring us?'

'We can ask.'

'Yes! We could borrow a long-range camera and sneak over. Come on, the ferry leaves in half an hour.'

But I'm standing rooted, gazing back at that hellish bungalow, watching grisly Jethro Dobbs returning indoors to his creepy wife. It's all at once clear to me. It's not enough to take pictures. We've got to rescue these animals. 'Why don't we forget the pictures?'

'What?' says Blaise.

'Just take the animals . . .'

'What do you mean?'

'Take them. Under cover of darkness.'

'You mean . . . ?'

'Sail over and spirit them away. What better proof of cruelty and neglect than to invite the ISPCA over to Peig's place and say, *Look, is this cruelty or what?'*

'You mean just sneak over and make off with the animals?'

Reaching slowly, like in a dream, for my inhaler, 'Yes.'

'What, all of them?'

Lungs rasping, 'Many as we can manage.'

Blaise gazing at me, looking back at the bungalow, and round at the island. Wildly excited, 'You're right, Lorcan! That's what we've got to do, take the animals! Liberate Inishbán! Find them new homes. Che Guevara, beat that!'

Starting back the way we came, buzzing with excitement, when suddenly I remember: 'TJ and Clinton. Don't fancy running into them.'

Scrambling to higher ground, Blaise trains her binoculars to the rocks below the graveyard. 'They're still there.'

'Come on, then! How do we get down to the ferry without going near the lodge?'

'We don't. We've got to sneak a look at the plans for the road, remember?'

Running now towards the mansion, my lungs complaining bitterly, chest teeming with demons, slowing me down and telling me, *You can't even run fifty metres – how are you going to liberate an island?* Damn you, demons! You try and stop me!

Through the garden and up towards the terrace we go. Carefully now, slowly. No sign of TJ's gran and sister, but his dad and Clinton's dad and the other conspirators are relaxing with drinks at the far end of the terrace. Smell of cigar on the breeze, champagne glasses winking in the sun. My breathing's really bad now.

'Blaise, wait a sec . . .'

'Sorry, I forgot.'

'No, I mean the plans – do we have to see them?'

'What! Pass up a chance like this?'

'Yes, but aren't we taking on enough?'

'Lorcan, you please yourself, but I'm getting a look at those plans if it's the last—'

Voices! Behind us! Coming up the track.

20

'TJ and Clinton – quick!' says Blaise, and we're off, flying up the garden steps to the terrace, where Mrs Gleeson appears pushing a lunch trolley.

'All done?' she says.

'Yes, zank you.'

'Run along then and catch your ferry.' Looking at me strangely, 'What's wrong with him?'

'Oh, iz OK, he has a leetol asthma.'

Jack de Barra's seen us. Blaise waves, 'Zank you so much!'

'Did you find your ancestor?'

'Yes, I zink so.'

'Good. *Adiós!*'

'Straight through the drawing room – you know the way,' says Mrs Gleeson.

Enter the deserted drawing room, we stop, glance over our shoulders, and then over at the dining table, where the plans lie unguarded. The pair of us hesitating, listening to Mrs Gleeson setting the table outside, and the voices of the men along the terrace.

Wheezing fiercely, 'TJ and Clinton could appear any second.'

'Stand guard,' says Blaise, skipping over to the dining area.

I can't stand. Best I can do is turn a chair to face the open window and slump. Peeking out, I can spy on Mrs Gleeson polishing a knife before setting it down in its correct position, and beyond her the men hobnobbing in the sun.

'Can you believe it!' Blaise exasperated.

'What's wrong?'

'There's pages and pages . . .'

Oho! Familiar blond head and dark head bobbing up the garden steps. 'It's them, TJ and Clinton! Coming up through the garden—'

'Just a sec . . .'

'They're coming! We got to go!'

'OK, OK! Come on!'

Blaise moves fast, and I'm trying to follow, but the lungs aren't working, legs going from under me, moving like in a dream towards the hall, horribly exposed in the open drawing room.

'You still here?' – Mrs Gleeson striding in from the terrace. 'What are you doing?'

'I'm sorry, I, um . . . dropped something.'

'Aren't you supposed to be Spanish?'

Breathless, 'No, I'm from here. Miss Santamaria's staying with me.'

'What was it you dropped?'

Can't speak, frozen by the sight of TJ and Clinton ambling past the window in muddy boots. If they see me, I'm—

'I said, *What did you drop?*'

'Um, a contact lens.'

'What, over there?'

'It rolled.'

'Wait here a moment.'

'It's OK, I—'

She's gone, out onto the terrace, calling, 'TJ, there's a lad in there lost a lens. Help him find it, else he'll miss his ferry. Leave your boots outside.'

Quick, move as best I can towards the hall, dragging myself on hollow legs – freeze!

'If that's your attitude, Nicole –' Mrs de Barra coming down the hall stairs shouting – 'I've a good mind to cancel your party altogether!'

Never make it. I'm trapped – Mrs de Barra in the hall, TJ and Clinton removing their boots before coming in. Do something – do *something!* Drop to the floor, crawl under furniture, sprawl behind a sofa, fumbling for my inhaler.

Footsteps padding into the room. 'Where is he?' TJ.

'Must be a midget.' Clinton.

Holding my breath, listening to them l
ing around.

'There's no one here, Mrs Gleeson!' TJ
shouts. 'Must have found it.'

Good, they're leaving.

No, they're not, they're coming closer, and
the sofa jolts as first one and then the other
throws himself into it, and they start tapping
away at pocket computers. Lungs on fire,
can't hold on much longer.

Out in the hall, Mrs de Barra seeing Marie
the hairdresser out. Footsteps, a woman's
heels, entering the room. 'Right, boys, get
washed for lunch.'

'Just a minute, Ma.'

'Never mind just a minute.'

'But I'm right in the middle—'

'Now!'

TJ clucks his tongue in annoyance, the boys
leave. Silence. Where's Mrs de Barra? Still in
the room. Here she comes, brushing the sofa.
Can see her white jeans and striped top, her
back to me as she heads for the window, re-
positions the chair I moved. If she turns, she'll
surely see me. And if she doesn't, she'll hear
my breathing any second now. Grateful for
the noise TJ and Clinton are making fooling
around in the hall.

She's turning towards a flower display in
the window, rearranging first one, then
another long stem. Pausing now, listening to

something – me behind the sofa! Turning her head . . .

Close my eyes tight, like a toddler who imagines a grown-up can't see him if he can't see her.

'What do you think you're playing at, young man?'

Heart stops. That's it – she's going to scream, call the police, have me dragged away accused of goodness knows what.

Open my eyes, ready to meet hers and apologize, something like, *Sorry, I was just having a little attack—*

But she's gone! Out into the hall in a temper.

'Do you want to go tell your father, Clinton, that you were swinging on my drapes?'

'Sorry, Mrs de Barra.'

'And you should know better than to let him, TJ! Honestly! Go get cleaned up, you've two minutes.'

Listen to the boys padding up stairs – Mrs de Barra's heels fading down the hall – laughter coming from the terrace. Pull myself up by the back of the sofa, ready to make for the door – when my eyes are drawn to the sheets of paper scattered on the dining table.

The plans! They're calling me: *Come and get us, Lorcan . . . if you dare.*

Madness! Can't believe I'm even thinking of it, never mind moving like a sleepwalker towards the raised dining area, wheezing as I catch myself against the table, glancing backwards to check no one inside or out can see, and start grabbing maps, frantically rolling them, fingers, hands, everything shaking – stop!

Drop down out of sight. Listen to the click of heels in the hall – changing direction – climbing the stairs, creaking somewhere above.

Up again, fighting for breath. The maps have been rolled before and roll again easily. Several elastic bands, thick as Napoleon's artillery, lie handy on the table.

Bending everything in two to get it all under my jacket, retrace my steps on rubber legs towards the hall and peer out. Can hear Mrs de Barra somewhere shouting, 'I've never known such a spoilt brat!' and Nicole wailing, 'Yeah, and who spoilt me?'

Venturing into the hall. Come on – *come on!* Stop!

In the corner of my eye, a distant movement – Mrs Gleeson in the kitchen at the end of a gloomy corridor.

Eyes glued to her as I slide along a wall, wheezing like a lovesick donkey – and break cover, a stumbling run for the vestibule, and out into sunlight.

Blaise spinning round, 'You OK?'

Gasping, 'Yeah.'

'I looked round and you weren't there.'

'Come on, we're in trouble.'

'TJ and Clinton saw you? They all know who we are?'

'No,' say I, trying to run, but my legs won't obey.

'What then – what happened?' Blaise taking my arm, helping me along the drive, down past the helipad – running, stumbling – fighting for air – no full-blown attack now, please!

'Did they question you, or what?'

'They're going to come after us.'

'Why?'

'The plans ... minute they see they're missing.'

'What do you mean, missing?'

'I got them.'

'*What?*'

Patting my jacket.

'No!' Gazing at me as we run, 'You nicked the plans?'

Mouth working – nothing coming out – keep going!

Boat's revving to go, ferryman jumping aboard – Marie seeing us, telling him to wait. Lungs bursting, *Come on, come on!* Clambering aboard, Blaise yelling, 'Thanks a million!'

Marie offering a hand, 'Hold tight now, don't want either of *you* to fall!'

Flop and *breathe*, nice and slow – sea and rolling sky, vision blurring.

'Take it easy,' says Blaise. 'I'll mind the plans.'

Curl up out of the wind, measuring the breathing, spray cooling my face. Drifting with the growl of the engines, screeching gulls, drifting . . .

Blaise nudging me, 'Reception committee – news travels fast.'

What? Where am I? Sit up and— *Oh no!* Blue light dashing through Rialto, turning onto the little quay above the dock.

Look at each other – what now? Swim?

Two guards in high-viz jackets approaching the pier.

'What do they want?' Ferryman squinting into the glare. Marie shrugs; we're shrugging too. 'Well, someone's been up to something!'

Boat docking, ferryman helping Marie off, walking to her car without a goodbye. Guards stepping forward, eyes only for us. One of them, jumpy and eager, helps me out, keeps hold of me – *Ouch!* Ferryman helping Blaise out.

'Don't let her go!'

Blaise: 'Hey! What eez going on?'

'Quiet!' goes the other cop, huge feller talking on a mobile. 'No need for the chopper, Mr de Barra, we got 'em! Hang on a tick. Open your jackets.'

Undo my jacket. Blaise unbuttoning hers, 'I said, what eez zis?'

'And I said quiet, young lady.'

'I am warning you –' stormy eyebrows – 'I belong to Amnesty International!'

'I don't give a fig what you belong to. Move a muscle and you're for it. Search the boy!'

Onlookers gathering on the quay while my cop runs his hands in and around my waist, up and down my legs and in my pockets – camera, dog chews, mobile phone, inhaler.

'What's with the dog chews?'

Fighting for breath, 'Sorry – my asthma.'

'Dog chews for asthma?'

'No, I mean—'

'What's the camera for?'

'Um, taking pictures?'

Big cop on phone going, 'How big did you say they were, sir?'

'What seems to be the trouble?' – Marie returning.

Big cop's going through Blaise's shoulder bag: camera, binoculars, make-up – 'Ah, it's you, Mrs Keating. We got a pair of thieves, here, according to Mr de Barra. Important charts.' Calling out to the ferryman, 'Search the boat.' To Marie, 'Did you see them up to anything over there?'

'No, Sergeant. Charming, the pair of them, and if you ask me –' cop bending to listen – 'Mr you-know-who's a bit hyper at times, forgets where he puts things.'

Big cop has hold of me and Blaise while

little cop and ferryman scour the boat, loaded with oil cans and bags of rubbish.

'I want every bag checked, every scrap examined!'

I'm looking at Blaise. Where the hell did she put them?

Second cop car drawing up! One of the guards getting out is female.

'Jeez, the whole flipping force!' laughs the ferryman.

Holding a screen round us while the female cop makes me drop my trousers, Blaise her skirt, and has a peek all around. Wait till Dad hears this!

Blaise blowing a weary sigh, 'I don't know why you are bothering with us.'

It's starting to rain; I'm starting to shiver.

Big cop back on the phone: 'Mr de Barra, I think we might have made a mistake . . .' – flinching as though stung in the ear by a wasp. End of call. Shrugs and looks at us. 'My apologies. Hop in the car, we'll take you home.'

'Let me,' Marie insists. 'We wouldn't want to go giving their families a fright.'

Cops gone. Blaise gets in beside Marie, I slump in the back. Away out of the village we drive, following Blaise's directions, and pull in a little way short of Blaise's house. Marie places her red briefcase on Blaise's knee, offers a tiny key, looks away humming. Blaise opens the case, lifting out squashed maps.

'I really didn't think you'd say yes, Marie.'

'Well –' rain lashing the windscreen, Marie gazing ahead – 'I don't want to see my lovely Connemara spoiled.'

'Thanks, Marie.' Big kiss!

One from me too, and we're out and running, past Peig's parked car and into Blaise's house.

'Da, we're back!' No reply.

Find Finbar and Peig having coffee on the covered decking out back, waiting for us.

'Ah, our swashbuckling buccaneers!' says a relieved Finbar. 'How was Operation Snoop?'

'Brilliant!'

'You got pictures?'

'Some.'

'Nobody caught you?'

Blaise and I exchanging glances. Peig hugging me, hugging Blaise, 'You had us worried, and I don't worry easy. Thank God that's over.'

Finbar's looking at us strangely. 'Hang on, Peig. Something tells me it's not over.'

They're looking at us; we at them.

'Come on, Blaise, spit it out.'

Blaise clearing her throat, 'That was just the scouting operation.'

'Why, what's next?'

'The rescue mission.'

Peig and Finbar's turn to exchange looks.

'Blaise was right,' says I. 'You've never seen anything as sad in all your life . . .'

'Worse even than I imagined,' says Blaise, and Peig and Finbar can only listen while we bombard them with all the terrible things we've seen – the flies and sores and skinny ribs, those wretched animals with barely strength to lift their heads, the hooves that haven't been trimmed since goodness knows when – on and on, desperate to make them understand –

'And the rubbish heap blowing stinking smoke everywhere and crawling with rats.'

'And the little mongrel – it'll be lucky to last another day.'

'All right, we get the message,' says Finbar, 'but what exactly are you planning?'

Silence – broken only by my breathing.

'Get a boat over – Gabriel's, if he'll do it. Grab as many animals as we can under cover of darkness.'

'And you think they'll come with you?'

'We made friends with them – the dogs anyway.'

'And take them where?'

'Well . . . we were wondering . . .'

'Yes, I can guess exactly what you're wondering,' says Peig.

'It's only a couple of donkeys, Auntie – a pony, a few ducks and hens, three dogs and, um, twenty-odd sheep.'

Finbar screwing up his eyes, trying not to laugh.

'You think you'd squeeze that lot onto Gabriel's boat?' says Peig.

'Well, maybe not all the sheep.'

'Maybe half,' says Blaise.

'The most neglected,' says I.

Finbar bursts out laughing. 'You two are hilarious.'

'What's so funny?'

'You never said anything about a rescue mission.'

'We only thought of it when we saw how bad things were.'

'When we realized,' says I, 'that a few

scrappy pictures wouldn't be enough.'

'The state of those animals, Da. We can't just—'

'Fine, I understand, and I'm sure Peig does, but listen, you can't just walk off with other people's ill-treated animals!'

'Not even to save them? Come on, Da, you're always saying we're not on earth just to have fun; we've got to be willing to stick our necks out when we see things that are wrong.'

'My dad says that!' says I excitedly. 'That if you see something wrong, you shouldn't look away. Never think it's someone else's problem – take responsibility. Worse than the bad man who does evil is the good man who looks on and does nothing.'

'Fair enough, Lorcan, I agree with all that, but this is . . .'

'What, Da? This is what?'

'Too big, too serious. You're twelve years old, for crying out loud.'

'Da, a year and a half I been watching those animals get kicked around, and I want to do this – I've *got* to do this.'

Peig throwing up her hands, 'You want us all to join your dad in jail?'

'It wouldn't involve you, Auntie.'

'What do you mean? You think we're just going to twiddle our thumbs?'

'*This*, on the other hand, definitely involves you,' says Blaise, pulling the maps from her jacket, slapping them down like a poker player.

'What's that?'

'The new road.'

Gazing at us, gazing at the rolled-up plans, 'You're having us on.'

Blaise shaking her head, Finbar reaching across the table – Blaise snatching the maps back, 'Not so fast!'

'How did you get them?'

'Lorcan nick – *borrowed* them!'

Jaws dropping, 'How do you know they're the real—?'

'We heard them – Jack de Barra, Willie-John McNulty and a couple of other suits, popping champagne and talking about keeping it quiet as possible, so objectors won't have time to react.'

Peig and Finbar stunned.

'Lorcan, hon, you didn't—?'

'I did! They were on the table as we left.'

'You mean you just—?'

'I couldn't help it, Auntie. The maps kind of sat up and said, *Take us!*'

'But they're bound to guess it was you two.'

'They searched us, getting off the ferry.'

'Who searched you?'

'The guards.'

Peig and Finbar look at each other. How much worse can it get?

'Then how come—?'

'Mrs de Barra's hairdresser – Marie Keating, who used to do Ma's hair, and who we helped earlier when she nearly broke her neck – Lorcan slipped them to me, and I slipped them to her to smuggle off the boat.'

'That was very risky and wrong of you both,' says Peig, shaking her head in disbelief; 'and very brave. I'm frankly shocked – and proud. What about you, Finbar?'

'Same. Shocked and . . . yes, Blaise's mother would have been very proud.'

'Doing good means breaking the law sometimes,' Blaise reminds her dad, 'like Countess Markiewicz, the Suffragettes, Jesus!'

'Come on, let's have a look at them' – Finbar stretching out a hand.

'First you have to promise,' says Blaise; 'Peig too – that you'll at least consider letting us do this rescue thing.'

'Fair enough, Peig?' asks Finbar.

'I suppose so.'

Blaise slides the maps across. Finbar and Peig hesitate.

'Go on, Peig,' says Finbar, moving his chair beside her while she removes the bands and spreads the maps. Mesmerized, the pair of them.

'Scumbags!' murmurs Finbar.

'Scoundrels!' says Peig. 'They want as much of the road as possible to run through bogland and wilderness, little as possible through farmland. That way there'll be less compensation to shell out, leaving the environment to pay the price.'

'If we're well organized, we can stop them, Peig,' says Blaise. 'I know we can.'

'To be honest,' says I, 'what's so special about bogs and wilderness?'

'What's so special?' Blaise appalled! 'They're beautiful, historical, mythical – teeming with spirits and stories.'

'Trees, plants and wildlife,' says Peig.

'They're thousands of years old,' says Finbar. 'They're the fibre and lungs of this country, our collective memory, and completely irreplaceable.'

'And all to knock a few poxy minutes off the journey,' says Blaise.

'If this goes on,' says Peig, 'we'll destroy what makes this country so special, turn it into a carbon copy of everywhere else.'

Finbar nodding grimly, 'Everyone too busy battling traffic to even notice.'

A shaft of sunlight falls across the table. The sky is breaking up – great pools of blue.

'It's up to all of us to preserve Connemara –' Blaise nailing me with her gaze – 'and up to you and me, Lorcan, to save those animals.'

22

Days pass. The four of us sit down to dinner
in Peig's kitchen – more a meeting than a
meal, with Brandy and Sadie wandering
in and out, pretending not to notice each
other, and Noel the crow sitting at Peig's
elbow pecking tea from a spoon.

Phone ringing. It's Doc Sweeney – word's
out that plans for the new road have been
leaked to the press!

'Goodness –' grinning at Blaise – 'wonder
who could have leaked them?'

'Might be on the news . . .' Finbar looking
around. 'Where's the TV?'

Blaise laughing, 'They don't have one, Da!'

Peig tries the radio. 'Listen!' –

Willie-John McNulty being interviewed on
the regional news is furious at suggestions
that he and Jack de Barra hatched a plot
to rush the new road through without
proper consultation. *'The ink has barely dried
on the plans,'* he insists. *'Of course I was*

241

going to make them public!'

'Ha-ha!' Peig and Finbar raising their hands, giving each other five!

Sadie resting her head on my knee – all this hullabaloo!

Back to the meeting.

'Finbar and I have given it a lot of thought,' says Peig, 'and I have to say, we're still not happy about—'

'But Peig,' blurts Blaise, 'I have to do this, I can't stand thinking about—'

'Hold on! Listen!' says her dad.'I was going to say that we do however recognize the spirit and maturity of your commitment, and feel it'd be wrong to stand in your way.'

'You mean we can go ahead with it?'

'Under certain conditions,' says Finbar.

'What conditions?'

'How about us coming along?'

'No! This is our thing.'

'We wouldn't want to get you both in trouble,' says I. 'A few animal-loving kids is one thing, but adults – wouldn't look good.'

'Well then, we'd insist you keep in close phone contact with us,' says Peig.

'OK, OK.'

'And I'll try and arrange for my vet, Tim Dorado, to be ready to receive any rescued animals.'

'Also, if you won't allow us along,' says Finbar, 'we suggest you recruit a couple more comrades to assist in such a demanding mission – with parental consent, naturally.'

'They're right, Blaise, we need more people.'

'Like who?'

'I don't know. Joseph?'

'Joseph! I can't get two words out of him.'

'We don't need chatterboxes, Blaise, we need men of action. And what about Róisín?'

'Róisín Kennedy? You got to be joking!'

'She's mad keen to join us.'

'She gets out of breath tying her laces.'

'So do I half the time.'

'And I don't trust Sticky Joe.'

'His name's Joseph and I trust him.'

'Another thing,' says Peig. 'What if Jethro Dobbs wakes up while you're relieving him of his animals, and challenges you with a gun?'

'Doesn't have one,' Blaise coolly lying.

'You sure?' says Finbar.

'Dead sure. Anyway, they start drinking in the morning, they're tanked up by mid-afternoon and completely legless by nightfall. They wouldn't hear if we threw a party.'

Peig shaking her head, 'Imagine what your parents would say, Lorcan, if they knew I was saying yes to this!'

'If we pull it off, Auntie, they'll be so proud.'

'Honey, they'd be proud if you were just dreaming it – but doing it? If something were to happen . . .'

Worried sighs.

243

* * *

Not easy tracking Gabriel, when he keeps
skipping acupuncture appointments, and isn't
on the phone. Best bet's the holy well, so back
and forth over the hill we go with the dogs.
Blaise still hasn't met Gabriel, only glimpsed
him disappearing over a stile or through a
misty gate.

It's Wednesday evening, we've hurtled
through our homework together and are off
on another Gabriel-hunt, when we step back
off a track to let a tractor go by pulling a
trailer crammed with lowing cows, gazing at
us with big innocent eyes. Cue for Blaise to
snap, 'There goes a load of your burgers,
Lorcan. Euros on legs. Blood money.'

'I'm sorry, Blaise, but to most people killing
cows for food is normal.'

'What, blowing their brains out without a
kind word? At least the American Indians
said thank you to the buffaloes they killed.'
She stands watching the trailer bump its way
along the track, the breeze blowing strands of
hair across her eyes. 'I hate this world sometimes,' she says.

'Come on, Blaise, one thing at a time.'

Nearing the little wood she says, 'If he's not
here this time, we'll just have to go round to
his—'

'Shhh! Listen!' Music on the breeze, and
there, down among the trees and jangling

244

tins, doing a little dance and playing his whistle – Gabriel!

'Listen, I got to warn you—'

'He's scary looking, you keep telling me.'

We can just make him out under the trees, lighting a candle, sitting still in the undergrowth. Getting up, lifting his bike onto the track.

'Gabriel –' running down – 'meet my friend Blaise!'

Staring open-mouthed at Blaise – cross-eyed and crooked teeth, twirly beard bright with spittle. Blaise staring back speechless.

'Gabriel, could you take us to Inishbán? The animals are being ill-treated. We want to rescue them in your boat.'

Eyes rolling. Scary smile.

'You like animals, don't you, Gabriel?' says Blaise.

'Mmm,' he goes, nodding madly.

'Will you help us then?'

Doesn't know where to look. Puts whistle to mouth, toots a couple of times and pedals away like the wind.

'Gabriel, come back!' running after him.

Rider slews to a stop, looks round.

Running up puffing, 'It's important, Gabriel. I have to know.'

'Portant, yis.'

'Will you do it, then? Help us rescue those animals?'

245

'Gable love all Goddy craters.'

'I know that. That's why we're asking.'

'Gable say yis!'

Away he goes, pedalling like a lunatic.

Blaise screwing up her face, 'Was that the skipper of our ship?'

Secret meeting in Devil's Glen – only nobody's here, place eerily quiet, faint shouts from distant playground. Where is everybody?

Sniff-sniff! Cigarette smoke, pair of eyes watching me from inside a gutted car.

'Bang-bang!' Joey shooting me with a rusty exhaust pipe. Clambering out, grinning, 'Did I frighten ye, Lorky?'

'Just a bit.'

Here comes Blaise down the slippery slope, Little Toad trundling after.

'You're late!' Joey sternly, hands behind back.

'Sorry, I couldn't find the refills for my inhaler,' says Little Toad.

'Camogie practice,' says Blaise.

'No excuses,' says Joey. 'See me after!'

Camogie's wild! A thrilling version of hockey where you pick up the ball and whack it. I haven't seen Blaise play, but I bet she's lethal.

Joey grinning as he takes a pull on his ciggie.

'And you a boxer!' says Blaise. 'Poisoning your lungs.'

246

Takes another pull and blows smoke a
'So what's all the hush-hush? What's ⌐
story?'

'Come here to me,' says Blaise, low and
mysterious. 'I been planning this a long time.
Lorcan's joined, but we need more men.'

Joey rubbing his hands, 'Me ears are
flappin'!'

'You all got to swear not to breathe a word.
I don't want anyone jipperding . . . jepperd-
ing—'

'Jeopardizing,' says I.

'– the operation.'

'Me lips are sealed,' says Joey.

'Scout's honour!' pipes Little Toad.

'Got to warn you it could be dangerous.'

'More dangerous, the better,' says Joey.

'A real adventure!' says I.

'Cut the wrapping and give us the gories.'

'Right,' says Blaise. 'Inishbán looks cute,
but it's a deathtrap. TJ's da lets his caretaker
kick and starve the animals. Don't look at me
like that, Róisín. I been lying behind a pair of
binoculars for a year and a half. And we've
been over and seen it with our own eyes.'

'It's true,' says I. 'You've never seen such
badly treated animals – weak and hungry and
covered in sores.'

'Loads have died in the time I been watching. The rest haven't got long.'

'Why don't you report them?'

247

'I have! It's not easy for inspectors to get over, and when they do, yer man says it's 'cos of some virus, and he only gets a warning. There's one little dog could die any minute, if it isn't dead already.'

'We have a boat and a skipper who knows the currents,' says I. 'A vet will be waiting to receive them.'

'In broad daylight?' gasps Little Toad.

'At night!'

'Night? There's a full moon coming.'

'What's that got to do with it?'

'Um, I could never get away at night.'

'Not even for a sleepover?'

'You mean lie to my ma?'

'It's her busy time with the B and B, isn't it?' says Blaise. 'She won't even notice.'

'What do you think, Joey?' says I.

'Craziest idea I ever heard.'

'You're not interested, then?'

'Sure – sounds a gas.'

'Will your parents let you come?'

'No, but I'll think of something.'

'Róisín?'

'My ma says no to everything.'

'Make her say yes for once,' says Joey.

'Anyway, I wouldn't be any use. I'd only get in the way.'

'What, helping guide the animals to the boat, soothing them, keeping your eyes peeled?' says I. 'Róisín –' making her look at me – 'we need four people. Will you join us?'

Gazing at me, fearful and excited: 'Yes!'

'Right,' says Blaise, 'sit down, everyone – in close, knees touching, hands joined.'

Joey: 'What!'

'Close your eyes! Hands joined, you two!'

Shuffling bums into a tight little circle, eyes shut and sweaty hands.

'Repeat after me: *We vow to stick together ... striving through thick and thin ... to save the animals of Inishbán ...*'

Our voices drift down the valley sounding silly – and splendid.

'What are we called?' says Joey, opening his eyes. 'We got to have a name.'

Blaise: 'I been thinking about – the New Citizen Army.'

'Out of date,' says Joey. 'How about the ILA, the Inishbán Liberation Army?'

'Sounds like terrorists.'

Little Toad perking up, 'The Full Moon Gang!'

'Sounds like werewolves.'

'The Sons of Che Guevara!' says I.

'It'd have to be the Sons and Daughters,' argues Blaise.

'Blaise's Midnight Raiders?'

'Gabriel's Secret Army?'

'The Knights of St Francis?'

Maybe we don't need a name after all.

23

Sitting side by side in Peig's practice with needles sticking out.

'Look, Gabriel, we're hedgehogs!'

'Dead dogs, yis!'

'Not dead dogs, Gabriel – hedgehogs.'

'Dat wot I said – dead dogs, yis!'

Peig removing the needles, inviting me – and Gabriel, if he's not too shy – to join her and Doc Sweeney in the kitchen. Doc Sweeney feeding Noel a biscuit, 'Ah, it's good to sit down.'

Peig pouring tea, 'Dispensing all those drugs, Brendan – no wonder you're exhausted.'

'Restoring health, I grant you, is tiring.'

'Suppressing symptoms, you mean? Look at my nephew – isn't he looking well?'

'Lorcan, dear boy, don't tell me you allowed your delightful witch-doctor aunt to prick you with needles?'

Leaving them to tease each other, wander

250

out front to where Gabriel's feeding Freddie the fearless pheasant a packet of crisps. 'Gabriel, you still OK about taking us to Inishbán? Gabriel?'

Too distracted to listen.

'The weather looks fine for Saturday evening. But we need to see the boat, and do a trial run. Any chance of tomorrow, say five o'clock?'

Gabriel's head bobbing, mirroring Freddie's jerky movements.

'Was that a yes, Gabriel?'

'Five clox, Gable showy boat, yis.'

Phone calls – first to Joey's mobile, which turns out to be his brother Tristan's, up on a roof fixing tiles in a whistling wind.

'Haven't a notion where he is.'

'Will you tell him to ring Lorcan – urgently?'

Then, bracing myself for the worst, try Róisín's number and, sure enough – Mrs Toad. 'Why would you want to speak to her?'

'My aunt wants to invite her to a picnic tomorrow after school.'

'Rather short notice, isn't it?'

'That's all the notice the weatherman gave, Mrs Kennedy.'

'And what did you say your name was?'

'Lorcan.'

Scarily long pause—

'We could pick her up from school, Mrs

251

Kennedy. Bring her back whenever you like.'

'Aren't you the boy I had the misfortune to encounter on the train? With that dreadful creature.'

'The pedigree wolfhound, yes – and by the way, I'm having a sleepover Saturday night, and was wondering . . .'

'A what?'

'When friends stay instead of going home late.'

Shocked: 'What, spend the night?'

'It's a way of getting together to, um . . . work on our school projects.'

'Young man, you're giving me a headache.'

On the headland with Blaise, lying flat watching Inishbán, when suddenly—

'Quick, take a look,' passing me the binoculars.

Aiming them towards Jethro Dobbs's place.

'Oh no, I see what you mean . . . he's swinging a stick or something and kicking out like a lunatic at the hens . . .'

Blood freezing, watching a weenchy figure lashing out at birds I can see but not hear panicking.

'Your phone, Lorcan.'

'What? Oh –' digging it out – 'Joey! Listen, Gabriel's showing us the boat tomorrow at five – can you make it?'

'Have to check with me secretary.'

'What?'

'Cool it, I'll be there.'

'I wish you could see this, Joey – Dobbs lashing out at the hens. And Joey – it's Saturday, Operation Swoop. Can you definitely—?'

'No worries – see ye.'

Settling down again to observe Dobbs on the rampage, 'I can't believe it, Blaise . . . Is it the drink?'

'Drink can't do that on its own. He's evil!'

'My mum says people aren't evil, only things they do.'

'She hasn't met Jethro Dobbs.'

Phone again. 'Róisín! Can you make it?'

'Yes! And you know why? She's so booked out, she wants to let my room – and I said, Ma, that's not fair, where am I going to stay? *And you know what she said, Lorcan?* Don't you have friends who want you to stay a night or two? *I'm free!'*

Bed early, but can't sleep. Peig had to go out to dinner tonight. 'You sure you'll be OK, hon?'

'Not a bother, Auntie.'

'Any worries, you ring me and I'll be right over, OK?'

Clock below chiming midnight. Moon's gone in, never seen such darkness. Not a breath of sound. Reach for Sadie's head, the comfort of her tongue licking my hand.

Think back over the day – the Connemara Commandos, or whatever we're called, meeting up in Rialto, Gabriel nervous of Joey, Joey and Róisín shocked by Gabriel's appearance, all of us a bit amazed by his leaky old lobster boat, with its draughty cabin and chewed up tyres slung all round for protection and the letters MAID OF KILRAINE faded to a ghostly blur.

Joey unimpressed: 'This a boat, or a mouldy old bath tub?'

'Wuzzy say?'

'Says it's beautiful, Gabriel.'

Gabriel's getting jumpy: 'Peepo washing us.'

'Nobody's watching, Gabriel, it's OK.'

Then Joey starts leading Ginny Jo on board, saying we'll need her for Operation Swoop. And we all look at each other.

'Joey, she'll only take up space we're going to need.'

'I'm not leaving her. She's never spent a night without me. Any case, her presence will calm the pony and donkeys.'

So Ginny Jo becomes one of the gang, and clomps nervously aboard, Joey soothing her as Gabriel pitches the boat into the stream, takes us over to Inishbán, along its rugged shoreline.

In closer, pointing, 'Goody spotty duck.'

'What's that, Gabriel?'

Closer still. 'See? Goody spotty duck!'

'I see it, Gabriel –' a sandy cove, secret jetty thick with algae – 'good spot to dock, but can we get down there with nervous animals?'

'Liddle bath, yis.'

'Path, you sure?'

'Ziggy-zaggy uppy down, no probbum.'

'You been on the island before, Gabriel?'

'Campy liddle Gable.'

'Camped here as a kid?'

'Many campy time.'

Back in port, double check he doesn't mind us changing the name of his boat, just for the mission.

'Little potty white paint,' he offers, and a paintbrush, everyone watching me lie flat and re-Christen the boat *Grandma* after Che Guevara's wretched vessel.

Still can't sleep. Look out window, and – *huh!* – what's that? Someone's out there, standing still in the darkest corner of the garden. I think. Or is the moon playing tricks, dragging shadows around – one which appears to be wearing a beret, looking up at my window? Heart hammering, pulse racing. Moon shines clear and he's gone.

Heart settles again, watch the sky breaking into pools of stars. Fine for tomorrow night's crossing, radio confirmed it: slack winds, clear spells. Full moon, according to Róisín, handy for seeing where we're going. Tiredness pulling me back to bed.

Huh! What's that? Someone in the room! No moon and it's pitch black, and someone's there – I'm nearly sure of it – pale hands and trusty beret, just inside the door, leaning against the wall.

Can hear him breathing, the familiar wheeze of an asthmatic—

Or is that me?

Reaching for Sadie again. If someone's there, she'll sense him. Only she's asleep. Whispering aloud, 'Is anybody there? Is that you, Señor Guevara?'

Can't see him any more. Maybe he's drifted downstairs, looking for the music and dancing.

Sound of a far-off car, high-pitched wail in the stillness – rattling up the lane, headlights in the curtains. Thank God.

Skylarks – 4 p.m. Four underage guerrillas training in the barn out back, where Peig and Finbar can't see us. Trying out worst case strategies—

I'm playing Jethro Dobbs, Róisín Mrs Dobbs, lying together on a bale of hay, pretending to be asleep, while Blaise and Joey creep up to rescue the dogs, all played by one actor – Sadie. But Joey has to ruin it, running into the barn – the Dobbses' bungalow – to slip a ring on my finger.

'Joey, what are you—?'

'Aren't you two supposed to be married!'

Blaise laughing, Róisín turning beetroot beside me.

'OK, here goes,' says Blaise, and here they come, creeping up on us.

Now Blaise is barking, '*Woof-woof-woof!*' pretending to be Dobbs's dogs, and I'm stirring, getting up groggy and cursing, opening an imaginary window. 'Shuddup, ye

stupid dogs! Go back to— *Hey!*' seeing Blaise
feeding Sadie a chew. 'What's going on?'
Stumbling out of a pretend back door and –
ahh! – Blaise trips me up. I hit the ground,
with Joey pinning me down, tying my wrists.

'Joey! You're hurting me!'

'That's for kicking them animals.'

'It's me, you fool, not Dobbs!'

'*Shh!*' Róisín waving her arms. 'They'll
hear!'

Rrrrrr! Sadie bounding over, knocking Joey
flat, growling in his ear and licking him.

Everyone falling about laughing.

'Come on, again!' Blaise clapping. 'This time
with Dobbs carrying a gun . . .'

It's time to sit round the kitchen table and
agree the aims of Operation Swoop. Blaise
wants to rescue *all* the animals, including
every last ewe and lamb, with Brandy's help,
even if it takes two trips, so when Deathrow
Dobbs wakes up and steps outside, there's
nothing stirring but flies.

Everyone's against her. Saving the dogs,
pony and donkeys will be hard enough, without trying to round up and transport every
duck, hen and sheep.

'Sure you don't want to rescue the rats as
well?' teases Joey.

'In that case, we'll throw open the pens and
set them free,' says Blaise.

258

Joey's not so sure. Ducks and hens wandering dazed over the island. 'Anyone could pick them off – rats, birds of prey. We'd be sending them to their deaths.'

'The ducks will fly!' says I.

'Not all ducks fly,' says Joey. 'You seen these 'uns fly?' he asks Blaise.

'Hard to tell. I've only seen them flap around in their cages.'

Finally we agree to forget the sheep, but find time to feed the hens and release the ducks, hoping the ducks can fly. Then Blaise remembers the pens are locked at night.

'Peig! Do we have any wirecutters?'

Early evening, the mood tense, Noel the crow peering down from his perch, watching the busy preparations, four of us studying maps, discussing timing and tactics, while Peig prepares risotto fit for an army.

Blaise edgy: 'Róisín, will you stop looking so worried! You're making me nervous.'

Joey's jumpy too, keeps going out to check on Ginny Jo.

'Remember to pack Rescue Remedy,' says Peig.

'What's Rescue Remedy?' says Blaise.

'Concentrated extracts of flowers. A few drops on your tongue helps keep you calm in a crisis. Handy for the animals too. And a

couple of mobiles. I want you reporting in
every thirty minutes.'

'Are Captain Lynch and Corporal Kennedy
permitted to carry inhalers, Auntie?'

'As your medical officer, my advice is to use
only in an emergency.'

'Who says you're a captain?' Blaise objects.
'I never promoted you.'

'Oops, sorry, Major!'

Darkness falling as we load backpacks with
rope, bandages, bananas for energy, corn for
the ducks and hens, bottles of water and
torches. A simple code is worked out: One
flash – *danger!* Two flashes – *get over here!*
Three – *all clear!*

'What about blankets?' Róisín making
everyone jump. 'For the animals.'

'She's right,' says I. 'Why didn't we think of
that?'

' 'Course I thought of it,' says Blaise.

Catch Róisín's anxious eye and smile.

'Straw for the donkeys,' says Joey; 'much as
we can carry.'

'Good evening, Nelson!' Peig putting down a
dish at the back door, shooing the big black cat
away. 'You want to get your nose pricked again,
Nutmeg?'

Watching this, and Prudence shambling
over to investigate, can't help feeling ill
– the thought of maybe being arrested,
taken into care, never staying here again,

Dad visiting *me* in lock-up.

Phone again: Mum on dodgy line from Rio, giving her hosts hell for not treasuring their rainforests – *everybody's* rainforests. 'Anything strange or startling, sweetheart?'

Yes! We're sailing for Inishbán, I want to tell her, *to free its animal population!* But why worry her? 'Not really, just taking a boat over to the island tomorrow.'

'Sounds fun! How's the asthma?'

'Much better, Ma, you wouldn't believe it!'

We mean to bed down early – nine o'clock for a 2 a.m. call to action – but by the time we've packed the cars with the equipment, it's already after ten. Joey and I will be sharing a tent out the back, Blaise and Róisín my bed, and Peig's making up the couch for Finbar.

Blaise complaining bitterly, 'Why do *they* get to sleep in the tent?'

'Honey, I've only one tent and two sleeping bags.'

'It's Countess Markiewicz all over again, left to rot in jail while her comrades are shot – just 'cos she was a woman!'

Strange seeing three of my classmates tripping through the house with tooth-brushes, taking turns in the bathroom.

Lying fully clothed between Sadie and Joey in the dark tent, breathing deep but steady, stomach sick with fear. Is this what soldiers felt on the eve of Waterloo?

Darkness and silence for miles around. Lie listening to Sadie's hushed breathing, Joey's throat scratchy with nicotine, an inquisitive moth – just visible through the canvas – brushing its wings along the outside edge of the tent. Thinking of Dad in his prison cell, maybe wishing he'd behaved in court, like I'm half wishing I'd never mentioned a rescue mission. Provided my breathing's OK, I'll be leading the way up the winding path from the jetty later tonight – or rather at daybreak tomorrow.

Moon coming out, lending the moth a huge shadow above my head.

Whisper, 'You awake, Joey?'

'Yep.'

'Nervous?'

'Nah.'

Moon goes in again, repossessing the moth's shadow.

'Yeah, just a bit,' whispers Joey.

'You think we can do it?'

'Nothing to it.'

'What if we get caught?'

'Bit late to worry about that.'

'It'll be worth it, Joey, won't it, just knowing those animals are safe.'

'Who says they won't send them back to Dobbs?'

'Don't say that!'

'Whatever you say.'

Ginny Jo's whinnying miserably. Joey sticks his head out. 'What's the matter now? God's sake!' he says, kicking off his sleeping bag, putting on trainers and crawling outside.

Breeze ruffling the canvas. Look out the tent window – Joey soothing Ginny Jo in the moonlight.

Drifting . . . drifting . . .

Huh! Suddenly awake – sitting up. No moon, no Joey, rain tapping the tent. Look out. Can't see a thing. No pony, no Joey – they've done a runner! A quarter of our army's deserted – the entire cavalry! Crawl out into the rain, drops big as stones – look around.

There they are, in the shelter of the barn, Ginny Jo standing still, eyes closed – Joey curled up at her feet in his sleeping bag. Can horses really sleep like that?

25

Someone pulling my leg. Peig in dressing gown. 'Come on, hon, it's time.'

Starry sky now, everything still, the moon riding a bank of cloud.

Milk and porridge steaming in the kitchen. Bit early for that. 'Get it down, you'll need it.'

Trembling as Peig helps me into her rain jacket with all its zips and pockets. Ticking off my personal check list – water bottle, phone, torch, sausages, the sling Peig fashioned out of an old towel to carry Little Dog. And my inhaler. Where is it?

Blaise and Róisín travelling with Finbar, me and Sadie with Brandy and Peig, Joey trotting behind. Road empty, mountains dark and watchful. Moon spilling light across fields – throwing them back into darkness.

'Oh God . . .' sighs Peig.

'What's wrong?'

'I must be mad, letting you do this.'

'It'll be worth it, Auntie – even if we only find one sorry animal a new home.'

Turning into a gravelly drive, Gabriel's house with the dishevelled thatch. No lights, no sign of life.

Peig puzzled – out we get, bang on door, look in windows, toot the horn. Finbar coming over, trying to tell us something. Gabriel's over there, sitting on a log, shivering in a thick woolly jumper. Peig going over, 'You OK, Gabriel?' Won't look up.

'He's afraid – it's not right.' Peig's tone suggests we call it off.

'Gabriel, don't you want to help those animals?' says I.

Head bowed, coat scrunched in lap. Blaise stepping forward, 'Gabriel?' Lifting his eyes. 'Can't do this without you.'

'Deffro Dopp, he shoo Gable.'

'He won't, you'll be minding the boat,' says I.

'Anyone gets a bullet in the bum, it's us!' says Blaise.

Peig: 'I thought you said he didn't have a gun.'

'Only messing.'

Gabriel clinging to Blaise's eyes, as I did in the ring before facing Clinton. Getting to his feet, Blaise taking his arm.

Mercifully dark down on the pier, moths

265

beating a solitary lamp, Inishbán lurking in mist across the water.

Hugging Sadie as though I might never see her again, praying my breathing will hold. *Damn you demons!*

The *Grandma* coughs up a stink of diesel, killing the silence. Ginny Jo shies away; Joey coaxes her aboard. Gabriel unmooring the boat, taking the helm – *putt-putt-putt* – breaking the smooth water. Waving to Peig and Finbar on the quay.

It's still dark. Moon and stars shimmering in the water; same moon that may be shining through Dad's cell window, touching his bed. Light breeze in the rigging, gulls silently accompanying us, dipping and rising – *putt-putt-putt*.

Kneeling in the bow, shoulder to shoulder with Blaise. Joey standing with Ginny Jo, Róisín sucking her inhaler and gazing trance-like into milky water, Gabriel straight-backed and focused at the wheel, the dashing captain. A spell has fallen on the boat. Maybe this is the best bit, the *blessed* bit between the preparations and the action, when everything is perfect, when everything is possible.

Chugging in close to the island, mist lifting from higher slopes, Lazy Bones kicking off his blankets. Breathing steady, everyone calm, Gabriel wagging a finger at currents jostling the boat, frustrating our approach: 'Shop paying dilly dames, naughty wodder!'

One moment lying in the palm of the sea, next sucked into rocky shore, holding our breath as Gabriel rides the swell into the cove, shoving us up to the seaweed-smothered jetty. Lassos a rusty spike, securing the boat. Heart sticking in my chest, breath quickening. The spell is broken; we're going into action.

Suddenly, a phone ringing! Up and down the rocky shore. Blaise pointing to my hip. My mobile! Wrestle it out of my pocket: 'Hello?'

'Where are you, honey? You OK?'

Whispered gasps: 'Auntie, you're not supposed to call—'

'You were supposed to call us!'

'We've only just landed.'

'OK, hon – call us in thirty.'

Joey leading Ginny Jo off, one slithery step at a time: 'Shhh – softly, girl . . .'

Clearing the slime, helping Joey strap blankets, sacks of hay and coils of rope to Ginny Jo's back. Shhh, all set. Everyone looking at me, eyes asking, *You OK?*

Fine! Thumbs up! Return Gabriel's wave – he's spreading straw – and lead the way up the sandy path, Blaise close behind, then Róisín – she's not Little Toad any more – and Joey bringing up the rear with Ginny Jo.

Darkness mixed with silvery light, moon slow-sweeping the island, setting shadows

267

running. Sheep looking up, startled, hobbling away with their eerily silent lambs. Joey swoops, grabs a sheep round the neck, whips out a knife and – severs the rope round its legs.

'Have a nice day!' he whispers as it takes off.

As planned, I'm running ahead, up and up to higher ground, scattering spooky-looking sheep. Throw myself down between moon-washed boulders, sweep the island with binoculars and aim for the spot where TJ and Clinton were fishing the other day. Not quite high enough to see.

Turn and pick out Blaise in the mist below. Point torch and give three flashes for *All clear*! But *is* it all clear? I'm only going on what I can see. We never worked this out properly. This must be how Che Guevara learned – in action, trial and error.

Wait for the others to arrive, Blaise glowing with excitement, Róisín stumbling and wide-eyed, Joey and Ginny Jo close behind, treading mist.

Blaise in my ear: 'Isn't this great!'

Pressing on around clumps of tall grass, over smooth rocks greasy with dew, and fling my sights once more towards the fishing rock, and – 'Oh no, it's still there!'

'The tent?' Blaise snatching the binoculars.

'What's w-wrong?' stutters Róisín, dropping between us.

'TJ and Clinton – they could be in that tent below, camping out.'

'Long as they stay there.'

'What if they're getting up early to fish?' says I.

'TJ and Clinton?' scoffs Blaise. 'I don't think so.'

'Jesus, Mary and Joseph, keep it down,' hisses Joey, working his way round rocks with Ginny Jo.

'I don't want to be looking over my shoulder,' says I.

'So what do we do?' says Blaise.

'Go see.'

'And if they're in there?'

'Crack their heads and throw 'em in the sea,' says Joey.

'Shhh,' says I. 'Get the rope. We'll tie them up.'

'I'm coming,' says Blaise.

'Right, Róisín, Ginny Jo's yours,' says Joey.

'M-me?'

'Stroke her face, talk to her,' handing over the reins and removing two coils of rope from a backpack.

'And keep watch,' says I.

'OK,' says Róisín, desperate not to fail.

Blaise gritting her teeth, 'Come on, it'll be light soon.'

She's right. The faint glow in the east is spreading as three of us tumble down the hill and then instinctively pull up and start tip-toeing towards the tent. Joey tosses each of us a coil of rope, moves in and crouches at the closed flap door. Bends closer, listens. Shrugs. Directs me and Blaise to place ourselves either side of the flap, slips a hand in, feels for the zip, starts gingerly opening and – *ziiiiips* it open in one violent move and plunges inside to leap on the two sleepers and terrify them into submission.

'Pity,' he goes, crawling backwards out of the empty tent. 'I was looking forward to a bit of vengeance.'

Thank goodness! I'm thinking. Rescuing other people's abused animals is surely illegal enough, without assaulting and tying up two classmates.

Back up the slope, lungs rasping but coping, blood pounding in my ears. There's Róisín, sucking her inhaler, frantically stroking poor Ginny Jo.

'She was real calm –' Róisín whispering excitedly – 'and I've not seen anything.'

'Good work, Sergeant Kennedy!' says I, promoting her on the spot. 'That is with, um – Major McBride's permission?'

'You got it!' says Blaise, slapping Róisín on the back.

Róisín embarrassed as she hands the pony back to its owner.

Press on to the cemetery, mist clinging to

graves, keeping their occupants warm. Round the ruined church and up to the track, moon running clear, lighting the way. Breeze carrying sickly whiffs of burning rubbish. Pause to look back and scan Clarendon Lodge, lurking in pale light above the mist line. All dark and quiet.

'Come on,' Blaise waving us forward. 'Look at the light!'

Darkness is rapidly thinning, night giving way to day, stripping away our cover. We're miles behind schedule.

Breathing getting thinner too. Not now, please! Patting pockets, where did I put it? *No! I don't believe it* – It's in the other jacket. *Eejit*! Means I got to do this whole thing without chemical assistance.

Ha! Just listen to the demons: *We got you now! You're going to collapse and make a complete fool of yourself.*

I'm not going to collapse. I refuse!

They'll have to carry you back!

Relax – *relax!* I tell myself; you can always borrow Róisín's. Or manage without.

You'll never manage without.

We'll see!

Round the final bend in the road – stop! A light ahead! Joey holding Ginny Jo steady, all of us staring at the small hanging light, trying to work out what it is.

'It's a window in the bungalow, I think.'

271

'No, it's an outside light,' says Blaise. 'I remember now: they keep it on all night.'

Moving forward, eyes peeled, towards the house. No sound and nothing stirring – wait! What's that? All of us frozen by the sound of a footstep! And another. Slow hushed footsteps on gravel. But where – ahead? Behind?

'Who is it?' murmurs Róisín.

'Trouble . . .' whispers Joey, lump in his throat. Never seen him scared before, and it makes me even scareder.

'It's coming from over there,' Róisín pointing a quivering finger towards the scruffy enclosure just off the track.

'Here comes your *trouble*,' chuckles Blaise as the outlines of two donkeys and a pony appear out of the mist, their gravelly foot-steps not footsteps at all, but the sound of their jaws weakly pulling up weeds.

Joey curses himself and starts unpacking the spare sack of hay reserved for this moment.

Blaise and I crouching down to watch the bungalow, fifty or sixty metres away, while Joey and Róisín lead Ginny Jo down to the enclosure.

'Where the hell's the gate?' Joey hissing.

'Shhh,' goes Róisín, glancing around.

Lifting their heads, the donkeys and pony give feeble cries of alarm, which Ginny Jo answers with a shudder of her own. Joey, carefully lifting the gate, leads Ginny Jo inside, and together with Róisín tries tempting the animals with handfuls of hay.

Up on the track, we watch and wait. The animals are frightened, turning this way and that to escape their rescuers.

'I better go help,' whispers Blaise.

But as she scuttles down to the fence, Joey waves her away. It's going better now, pony and donkeys are reassured by Ginny Jo's presence, or because Joey and Róisín are so much gentler than the animals' vile owner, or because they can't resist the sweet smell of the hay. Whatever the reason, they're allowing themselves to be led slowly, patiently out of the enclosure and up to the track.

Swap frantic signals with Joey and Róisín, whose task is to deliver the animals to Gabriel and return to us quick as they can.

Now Blaise and I turn our attention to the pens where the ducks and hens are kept, off to one side of the bungalow. To reach them without rousing the dogs, we move off the track, keeping to scrub and prickly gorse, bending low and praying the breeze won't betray our scent.

Reach the pens and peer in. From inside comes fearful quacking and clucking and the *tweet-tweet-tweet* of chicks. 'Shhh . . .' goes Blaise, attacking the hens' chicken-wire gate with wirecutters. Here I go, ducking inside

273

and tipping a bag of corn on the ground, and leaving several more bags for the hens to peck open at their leisure. Blaise is at my shoulder, pouring bottles of water into the hens' trough. What a feast! Close and secure the gate.

Look back down the track to see Joey and Róisín leading the donkeys and pony out of sight. Blaise grinning at me, giving me an ecstatic thumbs up.

Blaise now cutting open the ducks' gate, and I'm darting in to lay a trail of corn out into the open.

'Come on, guys, you're free. Fly away!'

If they can.

Leave gate wide open and turn back towards the bungalow. Stop and catch myself against a tree, like I did stumbling off that bus in Dublin the other day. Only this is a different me. My hands and eyes are the same, but I've changed. This is real and I'm scared, but I'm doing it. This isn't rubber bands and toy soldiers on the bedroom floor. This is me and friends occupying TJ de Barra's island, creeping up on Deathrow Dobbs's house.

'Don't flinch now . . .' murmuring aloud. 'Don't flinch, Lynch.'

'That's what we'll call you, if we get through this,' whispers Blaise. 'No-Flinch Lynch.'

'I suppose it's better than No-Puke Luke,' says I, and all at once we're bursting with suppressed giggles, bent over trying to keep it in, all the tension, the craziness of this operation.

Calmly now, calmly. Closer to the bungalow. No sound or movement from the dogs' oil-drum kennels.

No sign yet of Joey and Róisín. What do we do? We can't wait. Blaise blows a worried sigh as I take out the mobile, hold it up to the moon and dial.

Peig instantly: *'Tell us.'*

'Objectives one and two well under way. Closing in on number three.'

'Is Joey back with you?'

'Joey? Yup . . .' glancing at Blaise, 'he's just coming.' Daren't tell her he's nowhere in sight.

'Be careful, you hear.'

Closer now, closer, edging up to the fence, armed with sausages.

What's that? Something's awake, and it's not the dogs – rats scavenging for scraps. They're *huge*!

Moon's gone in, oil drums in shadow. Silence, apart from muffled quacks from ducks exploring freedom.

Low snarling from the nearest drum –

'Shhh, it's only us . . .' murmurs Blaise.

Both of us crouching, holding sausages to the wire. 'Nice dog, remember us . . . ?' More growling, sharper now.

'Breeze blowing the wrong way,' I whisper.

'What?'

'Can't smell them.'

Blaise rising carefully, reaching for the gate.

Ra-ra-ra-ra-ra-ra!

Damn! Young Dog springing up, barking wildly, intending to come bounding over, but betrayed by weak legs, stumbles to his knees. Picks himself up and lurches nearer, barking loud enough to wake Dobbs, his wife and half the country.

Ra-ra-ra-ra-ra-ra-ra!

No one could sleep through this!

'*Shhh! Shhh!*' Blaise offering meat over the tips of the barbed wire. 'It's OK, it's only us – here, look!'

I'm staring at the house, braced for the inevitable, when the demented dog catches the smell of meat and stops – sniffs, jerks back in fear; comes again, stretching his neck and – *snap!* – grabs a saussie and drops down, munching frenziedly.

'Take your time, doggie.' Blaise signals to me, *Come on in*.

Lungs scraping like blackboards as I rise slowly, eyes fixed on doors and windows. Dog looks up, growls.

'It's OK, doggie – here!' Toss him a sausage and follow Blaise cautiously into the garden, over to the old bitch, who gazes out from her

drum with milky eyes – She's blind! How u
we miss it? – and softly growls.

Whispering as I spread a blanket on the
ground, 'It's OK, it's only me – look what I got
for you.'

The stink inside her drum catches me in the
stomach as I leave meat at the entrance to
tempt her out. Mid-growl, she stops, sniffs
and drags herself forward, hunting frantically
with her nose and – *snap!* – got it!

Blaise still trying to win Young Dog's trust,
while I move quickly to the third oil drum,
where Little Dog, gungy eyes blinking,
flinches as I reach in to leave a sausage. Can
hear him sniffing and licking the meat, as if
he hasn't the strength to do anything more.
Where's his dish? Chuck away scraps of filthy
water, take out my water bottle, replenish the
dish and place it at the mouth of the drum.
Light flickering in Little Dog's eyes as he
stretches his neck to drink.

Young Dog vomiting somewhere in the
stillness.

'Water . . .' I whisper over to Blaise. Blaise
nods, empties Young Dog's dish and pours.
Young Dog snaps at her to drive her back and
dives in, lapping noisily.

Watching the house as I lift the improvised
sling over my head. Once Little Dog's in it,
and Old Dog's wrapped in the blanket, we'll
carry them off, linking up with Joey and

277

Róisín somewhere along the path. Lured by more sausage, Young Dog will surely follow.

Set down more meat on the edge of the blanket, and here comes Old Dog, dragging herself out on her belly. Blaise comes over to help, turning her back on Young Dog. 'Come on, bit further,' she whispers, and reaches to stroke Old Dog, who jerks her head and snaps blindly. 'Relax, it's OK . . .'

It's not OK, here comes Young Dog, staggering across the garden – *ra-ra-ra-ra-ra!*

That's done it! Lights coming on.

Ra-ra-ra-ra-ra – Young Dog barking dementedly.

I'm looking at Blaise; she's looking at me. Everything we practised goes out of our heads. A window swings open – Dobbs nearly falls out, crazy with sleep and drink.

'What the *hell* is going on?'

26

Both of us hopping back out of view. Blaise miming, *Get down! Get down!* She drops behind one oil drum, I behind another.

'You trying to wake the dead? Go back to sleep, ye stupid animal!'

Young Dog shrinks away, tail between his legs. Window slams shut.

Heart thumping, lungs breaking up. I can see Blaise clear as day, crouching behind Little Dog's drum. It's nearly light. It *is* light, pale and murky. What do we do now?

Blaise miming again. She's lost something. No, she's run out of . . . sausage! Right, toss one over. It's in the air – Young Dog onto it in a flash. Blaise scrambling over to help me lift the edges of the blanket, trying to *whoosh* Old Dog fully onto it. Praying this time that Young Dog won't react, but sick as he is, he's fiercely protective – *Ra-ra-ra-ra-ra!*

'Shhh, it's OK, we won't hurt her!' Blaise desperately trying to reassure him, but it's hopeless – the window bangs open again, Dobbs leaning out, Blaise and I throwing ourselves down.

'Shuddup, ye stupid cur!' yells Dobbs, and hurls something out the window – a bottle, which bounces up and catches Young Dog on the leg, making him yelp and run. 'Whatever it is, leave it alone!'

Praying he'll close the window again, but he's still there, breathing like a blocked drain. Has he seen the blanket?

Blaise miming again – finger to her lips and pointing at me. She's right: I'm breathing too loud. Try holding it in, but it's no good, I'm like a rusty old saw – *hee-haa, hee-haa*.

'Who's there?'

Blaise gazing at me, willing me to hold on. I'm trying, I'm really trying. If only Joey were here. Whatever made us imagine he'd be back that quick?

'I said, *Who's there? Speak!*'

Noises indoors, Dobbs banging around and then – nothing. Not a sound. He's gone back to bed! No he hasn't – *Crash!* Back door bursts open, just as we predicted in training, only we're not reacting, we're paralysed, and here comes Dobbs, looming round the side of the house in bare feet, hairy belly hanging out of his pyjamas and wielding – a shotgun! Down, quick!

'I know you're there . . .' Voice shaky with

nerves and drink. 'Come out, wherever you are, or I'll . . .' Nearer, nearer.

'What the divil's going on?' Shrill, groggy woman's voice: Mrs Dobbs leaning out the window wild-eyed.

'There's someone prowling around. Dog heard him.'

'Rubbish, it's the flamin' rats that pesky ferryman brings over. You were gonna talk to him, him and his filthy boat – the *Inishbán Rat Carrier.*'

'I'm telling ye, woman, someone was out here a minute ago.'

'Don't talk rot!'

'I'm telling ye—'

'Your head's full o' drink and divils.'

'*There!* What did I tell ye? I see you!' Kicks my drum and lurches into view, pointing the gun at me. 'Gotcha! On yer feet, nice and slow, or I'll blow yer head off!'

Rising slowly, 'Sorry to wake you, Mr Dobbs . . .'

'*What?*'

'I didn't mean to—'

'Wait a minute, don't I know you?'

Gazing into the barrel of a live gun.

'Talk, runt, or I'll blow you to bits!'

'Leave him alone!' cries Blaise, surfacing behind her drum, voice hard with terror.

Dobbs twists round, aims the weapon right at her: 'You again! I knew you two were trouble. What the hell do you want with us?'

While Blaise, mesmerized by the gun, raises her hands in surrender, the sound of a horse draws my attention to the track. Mist, which earlier was lifting, has gathered again, and over Dobbs's shoulder I can make out a pony and rider – two riders – Joey and Róisín returning. How do I warn them?

'Lost yer tongues, eh? Get over here, the pair of ye. Go on, move it! Down on yer knees, and hands up!'

Blaise and I kneeling, shoulder to shoulder, hands high. And here comes Mrs Dobbs, unsteady in dressing gown and scruffy slippers, face ghastly in the dawn, fixing us with a peculiar smile. 'What the divil are they doing here?'

'That's what I want to know, but they're not inclined to talk,' says Dobbs, leering at us with piggy, bloodshot eyes.

'That so?' says Mrs Dobbs. 'We'll see about that.'

'Put that gun away!' I hear myself cry.

'Aha, so we can talk!' says Dobbs.

'Not with that thing pointed at us,' says Blaise.

'What happened to your accent, eh, missie? Not so Spanish now, are we?'

'*Don't, please don't!*' I holler, praying the breeze will carry my warning.

Blaise throws me a critical look, but then

sees what I can see way down the track: pony and riders in the mist.

'I'm going count to three,' says Mrs Dobbs, pushing the gun aside with one bony hand, 'and you better start talking, or I'll take a horse whip to the pair of you, so I will. One – two—'

'We missed the ferry,' blurts Blaise.

'Missed the ferry? What's this then?' goes Dobbs, kicking a sausage out of Little Dog's reach.

'They looked hungry.'

'I knew it! It's about my dogs, isn't it?'

'And what's the blanket for?' snaps Mrs Dobbs.

'To sleep on,' says I.

'And that sheet round your neck?'

'Dislocated my shoulder in the cemetery.'

Young Dog skulks in the shadows, Old Dog crawls back into her drum. Dobbs glaring at us, Mrs Dobbs eyeing us crookedly.

Looking past them, I can see the pony and riders – have gone! The track is empty. Our comrades have opted to save the pony and donkeys and abandon us. Or . . .

'Why would you sleep here?' growls Dobbs. 'Why not at the lodge?'

'Because of my fake accent,' says Blaise. 'We'd get into trouble. You see, um . . .'

'What!'

'We didn't exactly tell the truth, Mr Dobbs.'

'What d'you mean?'

'We're n-not really interested in ancestors –' Blaise making it up as she goes along – 'we just like visiting graveyards.'

'Visiting graveyards?' cries Mrs Dobbs.

'And this one was high on our list.'

'What the divil do you get up to in graveyards?'

'Pray, light candles and dance . . .'

As Blaise rambles on, I catch sight of movement beyond the smouldering rubbish heap, pony and riders threading their way between rocks. And as they come closer, a plump little figure slides off Ginny Jo's back to the ground – Róisín, overcoming her breathing and terrors to attempt whatever mad thing they're about to attempt . . .

'. . . and sing praises to the elves for helping us, goblins for guiding us and the fairies for freeing our spirits—'

'Lies and poppycock!' says Dobbs.

'It's all part of our training,' Blaise insists.

'Training? What training?'

'We're trainee wizards.'

'*Wizards?*'

'I'm a white wizard, and my friend here's a . . . blue wizard.'

'What the hell are you—?'

'White wizards believe in fairies, and blue wizards in . . .'

'That's enough!'

284

'. . . ghosts and banshees—'

'I said *enough*!' hisses Mrs Dobbs. 'I'm calling Mr de Barra. See they don't move.'

'Wait!' says I, groping for another lie.

'You heard her,' says Dobbs. 'Zip it!'

As Dobbs stands over us with the gun, Mrs Dobbs turns away to go inside to make the call that will seal our fate. TJ's dad will drive over to get us – or instruct Dobbs to hold us till the cops arrive.

Blaise and I exchanging helpless looks.

But before Mrs Dobbs can reach the house – *CRASH!* The sound of breaking glass makes everyone jump.

'What the hell was that?' says Dobbs.

'A window, at the back,' says his wife. 'Quick – go see.'

'How can I, woman? I'm watching these two!'

Now the sound of a pony whinnying, hooves clattering on the track, and looking round I see an amazing sight: Joey on Ginny Jo materializing out of drifting smoke, charging through the garden gate at a full thundering gallop, straight for Dobbs, who twists round, gapes and lifts the gun –

'*No!*' Blaise and I scream together, bracing ourselves for the worst when horse hits man first, and Dobbs is lifted in the air, flung to the ground – thump! – the weight of him shaking the whole island.

Mrs Dobbs lets out an eerie laugh. Dobbs groans and gets to his knees, reaching for the gun. It's all happening so fast: Ginny Jo whirling round and charging again – Dobbs raising the gun and *BANG!* A deafening explosion rips the morning apart, a bullet flies into space and Ginny Jo neighs in terror – a blur of limbs and hooves as she rears and twists and kicks out a back leg – *thud!*

'*Aah!*' – a ghastly groan. Dobbs crashes like a tree and lies still.

Mrs Dobbs stands rigid, gazing at her husband sprawled on the ground, head flung back, eyes staring sightlessly at the sky, shotgun inches from his outstretched hand.

'Get it!' Joey calls, hopping down to see if Ginny Jo's hurt, checking each of her legs in turn.

Blaise pounces, lifts the shotgun, carries it gingerly to the safety of a window ledge. I'm kneeling over the body of Jethro Dobbs, heart beating sickeningly. *It was an accident, Your Honour, honest.*

But wait! The belly's moving, the eyes are flickering. '*Ahhh . . .*' he groans, clutching his ribs.

Joey's scrambling around the garden, nose to the ground, calling to someone out of sight, 'Get over here and help!'

The window-breaker – Róisín – appears

sheepishly round the side of the house, like she's done a very naughty thing.

'What you looking for?' calls Blaise, colour returning to her face.

'The cartridge of the bullet he tried to kill me with.'

'What for?'

'When the judge calls us liars in court.'

'Better call a doctor, Mrs Dobbs,' says I.

'Never mind a doctor,' growls Dobbs, sitting up holding his side. 'Call de Barra, woman – quick!'

Mrs Dobbs, shaking herself out of a trance, heads for the front door.

'The gun!' Joey cries.

But Blaise shakes her head, wants nothing to do with firearms. So Joey, pocketing the cartridge he's just found, moves quickly to block Mrs Dobbs's path. 'Where you going, missus?'

'To call Mr de Barra and have you locked up, like animals, where you belong.'

'I don't think so,' says Joey sadly, shaking his head.

'Get – out – of – my – way,' she orders, meaning to push past, but Joey reaches in his pocket – a blade catches the light. Mrs Dobbs gasps. Joey vanishes indoors.

'Get out of my property!' howls Dobbs.

Joey's back, holding up a telephone and its severed cable. 'Wanna make a call? Be my guest.'

'We'll have you for breaking and entry!' spits Dobbs.

'And vandalizing property!' screams his wife.

'And we'll have you for cruelty to animals,' says Blaise, tugging my sleeve. 'Come on! Work to do.' And to Joey, 'Mind the gun.'

More sausages and fresh water – and Blaise, Róisín and I take ages to tempt and coax Old Dog onto the blanket, noses twitching from the stink of her. Rolling her up, still growling, we lay her carefully across Ginny Jo's back. While Blaise stays with Old Dog, Róisín helps me lift Little Dog – trembling with fear and cold – snugly inside my sling.

'It's all right, Little Dog, you're going home.'

'Thieves!' Dobbs cries. 'They're mine – they belong to me.'

Young Dog's cowering in the bushes, Blaise waving sausages and calling him: 'Come on, doggie, come with us . . .'

'Wolves!' cries Dobbs. 'You're a pack o' wolves.'

We're leaving – Joey with the shotgun leading Ginny Jo, Róisín and I holding Old Dog steady over Ginny Jo's back, Blaise still pleading with Young Dog: 'Come on, dog, please.'

'And like wolves, you should be hunted down and shot!'

'Does it hurt, Mr Dobbs?'

'What do you think!'

'Good!' cries Róisín of all people. 'Now you know how these animals felt.'

Dobbs on his knees, waving a fist after us, 'Think you'll get away with this? I'll get my dogs back, don't you worry.'

'Leave it, you fool!' curses his wife.

I suppose I should feel sorry for her – but I don't. If there is a hell, I hope she and her husband end up there with Hitler and Jack the Ripper and those maniacs who planted the Omagh bomb.

Come on! Quick as we can along the track, me leading, phoning as I go.

Peig leaping into my ear, *'You've been ages – what's going on?'*

Breathing hard, trying to get the words out. *'Lorcan, hon – you OK?'*

'Fine – bit shook up – Dobbs came out and fired at Joey.'

'What! I thought you said . . .'

'Ginny Jo kicked him in the ribs – Joey slashed his phone – you better call a doctor – Second thoughts, we'll never get away . . .'

'What about his wife?'

'She'll have to run to the lodge – might just give us time – I'll call again.'

Movement off the track, Young Dog keeping his distance, head down, tracking us over rocks. Blaise and I calling softly, waving saussies, 'That's it! Come on . . . don't be afraid.'

Old Dog rocking on Ginny Jo's back, Róisín stroking her. If we pull this off, I'll have Róisín promoted to lieutenant! Little Dog, weighing nearly nothing, gazes up at me out of the sling, eyes thick with gunge.

Something overhead startles us, a pair of lumbering ducks in flight, heading for the mainland. Blaise cheers! *'Yeh!'* Róisín and I haven't the breath.

'Dead on!' cries Joey. 'Go for it!'

And still Young Dog stalks us through the gorse, each of us calling in turn, 'Come on, come home with us – you'll never be hurt again.'

The sheep have fled. You can see them flocking together far across the island. 'Still fancy rounding them up?' I call out.

Blaise returns a sad twisted look. Doesn't like leaving them.

Through the misty cemetery we go, down the steepening path on shaking legs. The moon has disappeared; dawn bathing the island in cool grey light. Joey flings the shotgun as far as he can throw it. Blaise climbs a rock and aims her binoculars. Young Dog chases after the shotgun, sniffing curiously.

'Get away from it!' Joey yells.

'There's Mrs Dobbs,' Blaise calls, 'heading for the lodge . . . all sobered up.'

Down to the cove as quick as we can.

Gabriel relieved to see us, standing proud in the boat, stroking the necks of the piebald pony and donkeys, who stand frail and shivering, close to collapse.

'It's OK, Gabriel, we just got to move fast.'

Róisín helps me lift Little Dog from the sling into Gabriel's arms.

'Gable moo fuss, yis!' he says, laying Little Dog in thick straw.

Joey and Blaise carefully carry Old Dog onto the rocking boat, lay her down beside the mongrel.

Gabriel shaking his head sadly, 'Paw craters, Gable mind yuz.'

Quickly now, Joey sweet-talking Ginny Jo aboard, the boat tipping in the swell. Young Dog watching from the bank, barking.

'Here, doggie,' Blaise hopping ashore to try one last time. But Young Dog bares his teeth and scampers away up the path. 'God's sake, do you really want to stay here with those brutes!'

'Blaise, we gotta go!'

A fearful roar and the boat sparks into life, spewing smoke. 'Crying out loud, Blaise, come on!'

Tearing herself away, leaps aboard. *Putt-putt-putt* – chugging out into the flow, Young Dog running up and down the rocky shore, barking frantically.

'Crazy dog,' murmurs Blaise, eyes shining. Turns away, can't look. Can't bear to see the dog's anguish. We all look away. Dobbs will probably kick the poor thing to death.

Suddenly – *Splash!*

We all whip round. He's done it! He's leapt in, thrashing around in the water. Quick – back again, Gabriel, before he drowns. All of us leaning over, pulling him in. Well, Joey mainly, and getting a bite in the ear for his pains. Young Dog, saturated and stinking, dropping over the side and digging into the straw with his mum. Joey bleeding like Van Gogh, Róisín tearing open the first aid kit, Blaise holding a handkerchief to his ear.

'Get off, stop fussing.'

Wide open sky and choppy water, a yacht with full sails gliding in from the sea. Wicked little waves beating the underside of the boat, and now the first rays of sun hitting the island where, even as we watch, Mrs Dobbs will be climbing to the terrace of Clarendon Lodge, shouting up at Jack de Barra's window, *We've been attacked – our dogs stolen – my husband grievously injured.*

I wonder if they've noticed the other animals missing?

Nobody speaking, everyone in shock.

Check my watch – twenty minutes since leaving the Dobbses' bungalow, and we're barely halfway across the water. Five animals

292

rescued, an unknown number of ducks freed. Not quite the liberation of Cuba, but not bad for a bunch of underage guerrillas.

What's more, we engaged a heavily armed enemy and after one hair-raising setback, in which half our forces were captured, turned a humiliating defeat into victory. Joey and Róisín's silent approach, the smashed window throwing the enemy into confusion, the decisive cavalry charge. *Magnifique!* as Napoleon might have said.

But listen! What's that?

Dun-dun-dun-dun-dun! – away on the wind. Everyone twisting towards the dreaded sound, looking at each other. Must be a couple of miles off, but sounds like it's under the boat.

Oh no! There it is, rising from the island like a giant insect. All of us watching mesmerized as the helicopter makes low sweeps back and forth across the island, hunting for us.

27

'Blaise!' I call. 'If he guesses we're in a boat, he'll head for Rialto.'

'Gabriel!' cries Blaise over the engines. 'Don't go to Rialto.'

Gabriel frowning; *what's that?*

'No go Rialto!'

The chopper's concentrating on the coast-line around the island.

Gabriel peering over animals' heads, 'Where Gable go?'

'Do you know any other ports we can put into?'

'Look, he's coming!' cries Róisín.

A moment's frozen terror – then action! 'Gabriel, how many ponies and donkeys can you squeeze in the cabin?'

Gabriel, wide-eyed: 'Gable skiz maybe two – fwee.'

Everyone scrambling round, pulling and persuading the two donkeys and the piebald pony into the cabin.

'Joey,' I call out. *'Joey!'*

'What?' Still holding a bloody handkerchief to his ear.

'Can you get Ginny Jo to lie down, cover her with straw?'

Joey nodding – do his best.

Gabriel leaning hard on the wheel, changing course, pitching the boat into waves rolling in from the open sea, the bow lifting and crashing, spraying the animals, making Joey slip and slide as he urges Ginny Jo to lie down and covers her in straw. *Dun-dun-dun-dun-dun-dun* – the chopper peeling away from the island, crossing the water, straight for Rialto.

'Down, everyone!'

Everyone dropping out of sight, crawling under blankets and straw.

Dun-dun-dun-dun-dun-dun – the chopper no more than a hundred metres astern of us, close enough for us to peer out and read J. DE BARRA – GALAXY HOLDINGS on the side, and to see Jack de Barra at the controls, looking this way and that as he aims for the yacht putting into Rialto.

'Gabriel!' Joey calls. 'Where else we can land?'

'Gable know liddle andy pot.'

'What?'

Blaise to me, 'What's liddle andy pot?'

'Little handy spot – or maybe port. What's it

called, Gabriel?' taking out my mobile and dialling.

Shrugs. 'Gable no-know.'

Peig: *'Yes, hon, where are you?'*

'Heading for a port, I think, past Rialto towards the sea – I see it! Tiny harbour, half a dozen houses.'

'I know it. Any animals?'

'Three dogs, two donkeys and a pony, all in bad shape.'

'We're on our way.' Can hear an engine starting up. They're sitting in the car! *'I'll tell Tim Dorado, the vet, where to meet you. See you soon.'*

'Look out!' Róisín calling.

'Down, everybody!'

Dun-dun-dun-dun-dun! Chopper arriving fast and low over the waves, rearing like a horse to get a look at us.

Peeping out, I can see Gabriel waving enthusiastically, one hand out of sight caressing nervous animals, while the monster hovers like a great wasp, thrashing the sea, sucking straw in the air – leaning into the clouds and peeling away – *Phew!*

Everyone kneeling up, spitting straw, watching the wasp turn its attention to a second boat heading out to sea, hovering above it. We can breathe again.

No we can't – it's returning!

Frantically rearranging blankets and straw.

Thunder overhead, sea boiling around u
DUN-DUN-DUN-DUN! Down for a close
look, blowing away our cover, the wasp
engulfing itself in a storm of straw. Terrified
neighing and whimpering drowned by the
din. Peeling away again – growing smaller as
it hunts along the coast.

Róisín looking green, panting like a fish as
she shakes her empty inhaler. Not breathing
so well myself as I move closer. 'Breathe
together – deep and slow.'

'D-did you see how I b-broke the window?'
she gasps.

'What? Yes, that was brilliant! We'd nearly
given up – and then suddenly – *smash!*'

Way up the coast the wasp descends over
Rialto as Gabriel steers us into a secluded
harbour, deserted but for a few covered
dinghies jingling in the breeze. Róisín and I
help each other off the boat. Blaise climbs a
wall, trains binoculars towards Rialto.

'It's landed on the quay! Blue flashing
lights, people everywhere.'

'Someone's coming!'

Muddy Land-Rover towing a horse trailer
pulls onto the quay. Man in hood and wellies
calmly gets out, opens the back.

'You must be Tim Dorado!' Blaise cries.
'We've just rescued—'

'Don't tell me! My job's treating sick and
injured animals. I don't need to know how

297

they got here. Come on, we haven't long,' he says, running to help us move the pony and donkeys carefully into the trailer, and the growling, snarling dogs up front with him.

'It's OK, it's OK, nobody's going to hurt you.'

You can see in his eyes he's concerned about the condition of the animals, but instead he says, 'Might be as well if you give yourselves up in Rialto.'

Blaise and I looking at each other – 'What do you mean?'

'Your dad and your aunt are being questioned over there right now. I'll be in touch,' he says, starting up the engine.

'Wait!' Blaise suddenly desperate. 'What will happen to them?'

'I suppose they might be taken to court.'

'No, the animals!'

'I couldn't say.'

'They won't be given back to that monster on Inishbán, will they?'

'Not if I can help it. Let me try and save them first.'

'Save them? You mean . . . ?'

'I don't know. I'll do my best.'

'I know a good home where they could get better.'

'I'm sure you do,' chuckles the vet, who's squinting now at all the blood on Joey's shirt.

'He got bitten,' Blaise explains.

'Better get him to hospital.'

Joey laughs – 'Hospital? Ye must be joking.'

'You're going to need shots.'

'Why, to put me down?'

'It's up to you. Good luck!' he says, driving off with our animals.

Blaise watches him go. I imagined her leaping for joy, but she's looking pale and sad.

'Now what?' says Róisín, slumped on a bench.

Good question.

Operation Swoop is over, but with complications. Peig and Finbar were supposed to meet us. Now they're in trouble and we're on our own.

'Could we climb the rocks to your place, Blaise?' says I.

'No, let's go to Peig's place.'

'You mad? It's miles,' says Joey.

'Do what you want, but my place is the first place they'll look for us, and I'm not ready for that. Anyway, I want to be with animals, want to see Prudence the pig, and Sally the goat and all the rest.'

'I suppose I better get home,' says Róisín.

'Me too,' says Joey.

'I think we should stick together,' says I.

'Yes!' says Róisín. 'I don't want to go home. I don't care if she shouts at me. I don't care if she grounds me – for ever! I helped rescue those animals . . . didn't I?' – looking for reassurance.

'You were fantastic!' says I. 'What about you, Joey?'

Joey sniffs, frowns – 'Mmm . . . I might just tag along for a bit.'

Gabriel's standing on the quay looking lost. Blaise runs over, takes his hands. He lowers his eyes, mortified. 'Thanks, Gabriel, you've been brilliant. You've allowed me to fulfil a dream.'

Gabriel squirms, studies his feet.

'Better go sail your boat, Gabriel,' says I; ''till things blow over.'

'There's a bus!' cries Róisín.

Round the bend it comes: BALLYCONNEELY VIA KILRAINE.

'That'll do!' yells Blaise.

I can't run, nor can Róisín – we're breathing like two slugged-out boxers. Blaise sprints, waves the bus down, begs the driver to wait.

'What are you all doing this time of the morning?'

'Dangerous mission,' says Blaise. 'Top secret.'

One small problem: I don't seem to have any cash. Nor has Róisín. Blaise patting empty pockets.

'Joey, you got any money?'

'What a load o' muppets!' says Joey, flicking open his wallet.

All aboard the nearly empty bus, except

300

Joey, trotting behind on Ginny Jo, kicking up a gallop when the bus speeds up.

Rumbling towards Rialto, sinking down in our seats, we can see Jack de Barra's chopper in the car park, cop cars on the quay with blue lights slowly whirring. Getting closer, peering over windowsills, we can see guards standing around on the pier – and look! There's Peig and Finbar chatting to Jack de Barra. No! Definitely not chatting.

'Skin and hair flying!' cries Róisín.

Peig's flinging her arms about; Jack de Barra's pointing an accusing finger.

'Look at my da,' cries Blaise, 'laughing in his face!'

The bus trundles through Rialto. Blaise seizes my arm. 'Will they get jailed because of us?'

'I don't think so, not when they see the state of the animals. But we could be in big trouble!'

'I don't mind,' says Blaise, looking out at the rolling clouds, the shifting sea. 'I want people to know about monsters like Jethro Dobbs, and swine like Jack de Barra who protect them. And I want people to know there are kids like us willing to get off our bums and do something.'

All stumble off in the dozy outskirts of Kilraine. Wait for Joey to come clattering up the hill, and find the road Peig brought me along the first night. Róisín's breathing like a rusty violin: we lift her up on Ginny Jo and set off walking. Three or four miles to go; the sun's gone, a keen wind picking up off the sea. Walking along beating ourselves to keep the blood flowing. Tiredness hitting us all together, the zip's gone out of us, trudging wearily like escaped prisoners. Heavy black cloud rearing up over the mountains, needles of rain.

Lungs bursting. Pause for breath and find myself thinking of Dad, how worried he was I'd turn out like every other brain-washed Coca-Cola kid trooping to McDonald's in Nike trainers.

Enjoy your Connemara adventure . . . and whatever you do, be yourself.

Blaise stroking Ginny Jo's face, 'We beat them, Ginny Jo! We did it!'

Silver rain spiking the fields, the road, lashing the roof of a barn down a muddy lane. Rain running down our necks.

'I'm flipping freezing, lads,' says Blaise.

'Are you?' says Joey.

'Aren't you?

'Are you jokin'?' he goes, teeth clacking.

All of us eyeing the barn, pushing the gate open, splashing down the lane. Slide open a big old squeaky door. Inside – a cathedral of hay and hush, rain smacking the roof. Ladder straight up to a gloomy hanging loft.

Ginny Jo presses her nose into the nearest

hay and gives a contented shiver. Up the
ladder we climb and dive into mountains of
dried meadow. Sweet smell of summer!

Fingers of light poking through cracks in
the wall. Hearts beating, breath pumping—

Blaise lying back, hands behind her head,
gazing into space; Joey leaning on an elbow,
ear clotted with dried blood, chewing a stick
of grass.

Róisín weeping softly, me holding her hand.

Eyes getting heavy . . . nothing left to say or
do.

Drifting . . . drifting . . .

Spoofer Rooney

by Jonathan Kebbe

Hopper's a hoaxer, a dreamer, an inventor of
crazy stories. Just listen to him!

Holy Spokes! There's a strange man living in me da's shed!

Is this just Hopper trying to get attention because his
ma is gone and his da's in hospital and he wants to
impress his scarily pretty cousin Geri May? Or is he
really harbouring a desperate fugitive, and could this
mysterious foreigner help him save his daddy's motor
repair business, and prove to the world he's not the
eejit they all think he is?

'An uplifting book in which the
volatile family feuds of an older gen-
eration are repaired by the energies
and optimism of youth'
Times Educational Supplement

ISBN 0 440 864682